JOHN MORTIMER

THREE CASES FOR RUMPOLE

Edited by: Solveig Odland

Illustrations by: Solveig Odland

The vocabulary is based on
Michael West: A General Service List of
English Words, revised & enlarged edition 1953
Pacemaker Core Vocabulary, 1975
Salling/Hvid: English-Danish Basic Dictionary, 1970
J. A. van Ek: The Threshold Level for Modern Language
Learning in Schools, 1976

Cover layout: Mette Plesner
Cover illustration: Solveig Odland
Consultant: John P. Folker

ASCHEHOUG A/S 1994
ISBN Denmark 87-11-08715-3

Printed by Sangill Bogtryk & offset

JOHN MORTIMER

himself a barrister, was born 1923. Educated in Harrow and Oxford he was called to the Bar in 1948.

He established his reputation as a dramatist with his play The Dock Brief (1958). Other plays include Two Stars for Comfort (1962), The Judge (1967) and the autobiographical A Voyage Round My Father (1970).

Mortimer has written many film scripts as well as radio and television plays including the adaptation of Evelyn Waugh's Brideshead Revisited (1981).

His bestselling novels Summer's Lease, Paradise Postponed and Titmuss Regained have been successful television series and the famous Rumpole stories, for example Rumpole of the Bailey (1978), Rumpole à la Carte (1990) and Rumpole on Trial (1992) have become extremely popular, especially through television. Mortimer was awarded the prize British TV Writer of the Year in 1980.

Editor's note:

Cockney

The original version of the Rumpole stories contains some non-standard grammar and expressions typical of Cockney speaking Londoners. Most of it has been kept in this Easy Reader edition for the sake of atmosphere.

Law in England

A **lawyer** is a person whose business it is to advise people in matters of law and represent them in court.

A **solicitor** is a lawyer who prepares legal papers for a **barrister** who may not accept a brief without instruction from a solicitor. The solicitor's functions include legal and business advice and drafting of wills.

A **barrister** is a lawyer who has the right of speaking in the higher courts. **Counsel** is a barrister or a body of legal advisers engaged in the trial of a case in court where they wear a wig and a gown. No partnership is allowed between counsel.

Q.C., Queen's Counsel is a barrister appointed to a senior rank on recommendation of the **Lord Chancellor**, the head of the English legal system. A Q.C. wears a silk gown within the bar, and takes presidence over junior barristers.

A **magistrate** is an official who has the power to judge cases in the lowest courts of law, especially a police court.

Rumpole and the Children of the *Devil*

Sometimes, when I have nothing better to occupy my mind, when I am sitting in the bath, for instance, or when I am in the corner of Pommeroy's Wine Bar having a glass of *Château Fleet Street*, I wonder what I would have done if I had been God. I mean, if I had been *creating* the world in the first place, would I have put together a world totally without the *minus quantities* we have grown used to, a place with no diseases, no traffic problems or Mr Justice Graves – and one or two others I could mention? And, when I came to think rather further along these lines, it seems to me that a world without evil might possibly be a dull world – and it would certainly be a world which would leave Rumpole and everyone else in *Chambers* without work. It would also put the *Old Bill* and most of Her Majesty's judges and prison officers out of work. So perhaps a world where everyone runs about doing good to each other is not such a wonderful idea after all.

Thinking a little further on this business of evil, it

devil, evil spirit
Château Fleet Street, château is French for castle.
French wines are often named after the "château" where they are produced. A cheap table wine is here amusingly given a fancy name.
create, cause to exist
minus quantities, bad sides
Chambers, a set of rooms used by a group of *barristers*. A barrister is a *lawyer* who has the right of speaking in the higher courts of law. A lawyer is a person whose business it is to advise people about law and to represent them in court.
Old Bill, the police

seems to me that the world is fairly equally divided between those who see it everywhere because they are always looking for it and those who hardly notice it at all. Sometimes, however, the signs of evil are so striking that 5 they are impossible to *ignore* as in the start to the case which I will call "the Children of the Devil". They led to a serious *inquiry* into the *machinations* of *Satan* in the *Borough* of Crockthorpe.

Crockthorpe is a large, rather poor area south of the 10 Thames. The people who live there speak many languages, many are without jobs, many employed in *legal* and not so legal businesses – among the latter the huge Timson *clan*. The Timsons, as those of you who have followed my legal work in detail will know, provide not 15 only the bread and *marge* but quite often the beef and butter of our life in Froxbury Mansions, Gloucester Road. Part of my intake of Château Thames Embankment, and my wife Hilda's gin and tonic, comes thanks to the activities of the Timson family. They are such a 20 large group, their crime rate is so high and their success rate so low, that they are perfect *clients* for an Old Bailey

ignore, not to take notice of
inquire, to try to find information by asking questions;
inquiry, the act of inquiring
machination, plan with an evil purpose
Satan, the Devil, the spirit of evil
borough, one of the local government districts into which Greater London is divided
legal, allowed by the law; concerned with or used in the law
clan, tribe; group of families
marge, (slang) margarine, a butter-like substance cheaper than butter; *slang*, words and phrases used in everyday speech, not for formal use
client, person who receives professional advice from a lawyer

hack. They go in for *theft*, shopbreaking and receiving stolen property but they have never produced a Master *Crook*. If you are looking for crimes out of the ordinary, the Timsons won't provide them or, at least they didn't until the day that Tracy Timson, so it seemed, made a *pact* with the Devil. 5

The story began in the playground of Crockthorpe's Stafford Cripps Junior School. The building had not been much repaired since it was built in the early days after the war, and the playground had been kicked to pieces by *generations* of under-twelves. It was during the mid-morning break that evil appeared. The children were out fighting, grouping together, or being unhappy because they had no one to play with. Among the most active, and about to pick a fight with a far larger black boy, was Dominic Molloy, *angel-faced* and Irish, who will figure in this story. 10 15

Well, as I say, it was half-way through the break. The *headmistress*, a certain Miss Appleyard, was walking across the playground, trying to work out how to make fifty copies of The Little Green Reading Book go round two hundred pupils. Suddenly she heard the sound of *eerie* and *high-pitched* screaming coming from one of the doors that led on to the playground. 20

hack, person who does hard and dull work, often for low wages
theft, (an act of) stealing
crook, person who is not honest; thief; criminal
pact, deal
generation, people born at about the same time
angel-faced, sweet-looking as of a child who can never do anything bad
headmistress, woman in charge of a school
eerie, causing fear
high-pitched, (of sound) high and sharp

The masks have horns

Turning towards the sound, Miss Appleyard saw a strange sight. A small group of children, about nine of them, all girls and all screaming, came rushing forward. Who they were was, at this moment, a mystery to the
5 headmistress for each child wore a *mask*. Above the dresses and the jeans and *pullovers* hung the red and black evil faces of nine devils.

At this sight even the bravest of the children in the playground were frightened and some of the younger
10 ones began screaming, too. Only young Dominic Molloy, it has to be said, stood his ground and even looked amused. Miss Appleyard stepped forward without fear. When the little group stopped she took off the devil's mask of their leader and saw the small, heart-shaped face
15 of the eight-year-old Tracy, almost the youngest of the Timson family.

Events thereafter took an even more *sinister* turn. At first the headmistress looked angry, took away all the masks and ordered the children back to the classroom,
20 but didn't speak to them again about the strange affair. Unfortunately she laid the matter before the proper *authority*, which in this case was the Social Services and *Welfare* Department of the Crockthorpe Council. So the wheels were set in motion that would end up with young
25 Tracy Timson being taken into what is laughingly known

mask, see picture, page 8
pullover, see picture, page 8
sinister, suggesting or warning of evil
authority, person or group with the power and right to control and command in public affairs
welfare, well-being; here the department that takes care of people in need

as care, this being the *punishment* for children who do not act according to the rules of the *conventional* society.

In my *childhood* there were no social workers. Now British children must *dread* the knock at the door, the footsteps of the Old Bill up the stairs, and being taken 5 away from their nearest and dearest by a member of the *alleged* caring professions.

The dreaded knock came at six-thirty one morning on the door of the *semi* in Morrison Close, where that young couple Cary and Rosemary (known as Roz) Timson lived 10 with Tracy, their only child. There was a police car with its blue light outside the house and a woman police *constable* in uniform on the step. A social worker named Mirabelle Jones knocked on the door. She was a perfectly pleasant-looking girl. When she talked she added a 15 working-class *accent* to her natural upper-class language. She always referred to the parents of the children who came into her possession as Mum and Dad and spoke with friendliness and deep concern. When the knock sounded, Tracy was asleep in the company of someone 20 known as *Barbie doll*. Cary Timson came down the stairs with heavy steps, certain that the knock was in some way connected with the break-in at a shop in Gunston

punishment, the act of making someone suffer for a crime or a fault
conventional, according to the accepted standards of manners
childhood, the time of being a child
dread, fear greatly
allege, to state or declare without proving
semi, half; here, *semi-detached* (of a house), joined to another house on one side
constable, police officer of lowest rank
accent, special way of talking in a particular area
Barbie doll, see picture, page 12

Barbie doll

Avenue. He had been called in for questioning several times, although on each occasion he had made it clear that he knew absolutely nothing about it.

By the time he had pulled open the door his wife, Roz, had appeared on the stairs behind him, so she was able to hear Mirabelle telling her husband that she had 'come about young Tracy'. From the statements which I was able to read later it appears that the conversation then went on something like this. Roz cried out 'Tracy? What about our Tracy? She's asleep upstairs. Isn't she asleep upstairs?'

'Are you Mum?' Mirabelle then asked.

'What do you mean, am I Mum? Course I'm Tracy's mum. What do you want?' Roz clearly spoke with a rising *hysteria* and Mirabelle's reply sounded, as always, *reasonable*. 'We want to look after your Tracy, Mum. We feel she needs rather special care. I'm sure you're both going to help us.'

Roz was not fooled by the pleasant voice. She got the awful message and the shock of it brought her coldly to her senses. 'You come* to take Tracy away, haven't you?'

hysteria, state of being extremely excited, out of control
reasonable, having/acting with good sense
*Cockney (see note, page 3)

And before the question was answered she shouted, 'You're not *bloody* taking her away!'

'We just want to do the very best for your little girl. That's all, Mum.' Mirabelle produced a dreaded and official-looking paper. We do have a court order. Now shall we go and wake Tracy up? Ever so gently.'

A terrible scene followed. Roz fought for her child and had to be held back at first by her husband and then by the uniformed officer who was called in from the car. The Timsons were told that they would be able to *argue* the case in court. The woman police officer helped pack a few clothes for Tracy. As the child was removed from the house, Mirabelle took the Barbie doll from her, explaining that it was bad for children to have too many things that reminded them of home. So young Tracy Timson was taken into custody and her parents came nearer to heartbreak than they ever had in their lives. Throughout it all it's fair to say that Miss Mirabelle Jones *behaved* with the *tact* and consideration which made her such a star of the Social Services and such a dangerous witness in the *Juvenile Court*.

Tracy Timson was removed to a dark Victorian house now known as the Lilacs, Crockthorpe Council Children's Home, where she will stay for the rest of this story. Mirabelle set out to interview the other kids Tracy was at school with. In the course of her activities, she called at another house in Morrison Close where young

bloody, (slang) word used to express anger or a low opinion
argue, to give reasons for or against something; to discuss
behave, act (in a certain way)
tact, sense of how to handle people or affairs so as not to hurt anybody's feelings
Juvenile Court, special court for young people who break the law

Dominic Molloy's father and mother lived.

Now, anyone who knows anything about the world we live in, anyone who keeps his or her ear to the ground and picks up as much information as possible about the
5 family *rivalry* in the Crockthorpe area, will know that the Molloys and the Timsons are as deadly *rivals* as the Montagues and the Capulets*. The Molloys are an extended family; they are also *villains* but of a more purposeful variety. To the Timsons' record of small-time
10 stealing the Molloys added wounding, serious bodily harm and a murder.

Now Mirabelle called on the eight-year-old Dominic Molloy and, after a meeting with him and his parents, he agreed to help her with her inquiries. This, in turn, led
15 to a further interview in an office at the school with young Dominic which was *videotaped*.

I remember my first *conference* with Tracy's parents, because on that morning Hilda and I had a slight difference of opinion on the subject of the *Scales of Justice*
20 Ball. This somewhat dull occasion is announced once a year on an expensive card which arrived on the Rumpole breakfast table together with the gas bill.

I had thrown this invitation away when Hilda, whose *eagle eye* misses nothing, immediately picked it up and

rivalry, the state of being *rivals*
rival, one who struggles to gain advantage over another
*the two rivalling families in "Romeo and Juliet" by Shakespeare
villain, person with a bad character
videotape, to record on a tape carrying pictures and sound
conference, here, meeting between a lawyer and his client
eagle eye, sharp eye-sight (as that of an *eagle*, a large bird that seizes and eats animals)

Scales of Justice

said sharply, 'And why are you throwing this away, Rumpole?'

'You don't want to go, Hilda,' I told her. 'Not a pretty sight, Her Majesty's judges jumping around on the floor of the Savoy Hotel. You wouldn't enjoy it.' 5

'I suppose not, Rumpole. It's too *humiliating* for me when other *chaps* in Chambers lead their wives out on to the floor.'

'Not a pretty sight, I have to agree, the waltzing Ballards and Erskine-Browns.' 10

'Why do you never lead me out on to the dance floor, Rumpole?' She asked me the question direct. 'I sometimes dream about it. We're at the Scales of Justice Ball. At the Savoy Hotel. And you lead me out on to the floor, as the first lady in Chambers.' 15

'You are, Hilda,' I hurried to agree with her, 'you're no doubt the *senior* ... '

'But you never lead me out, Rumpole! We have to sit there, staring at each other across the table, while all around us couples are dancing the night away.' 20

humiliating, giving someone the feeling of being of less value than others
chap, fellow
senior, older in years or higher in rank

'I have many *talents*, Hilda, but I'm not a great dancer. Anyway, we don't get much practice at dancing down the Old Bailey.'

'Oh, it doesn't matter. When is the ball? Marigold Featherstone told me but I can't quite remember.' She was checking the invitation to answer her question. 'November the 18th! It just happens to be my birthday. Well, we'll stay at home, as usual. At least I won't have to sit and watch other happy people dancing together.' And now Hilda was nearly crying. 'Go along now,' she said. 'You've got to get to work. Work's the only thing that matters to you. You'd rather defend a *murderer* than dance with your wife.'

'Well, yes. Perhaps,' I had to admit. 'Look, do cheer up, old thing. Please.' As I moved to the door she said, 'Old, yes, I suppose. We're both too old for a party. And I'll just have to get used to the fact that I didn't marry a dancer.'

'Sorry, Hilda.'

So I left She Who Must Be Obeyed, sitting alone in the kitchen and looking, as I thought, truly unhappy. I pulled myself together and pointed myself in the direction of my Chambers in the Temple, where I knew I had a conference with a couple of Timsons in what I imagined would be no more than a *routine* case of *petty* theft.

I had acted for Cary before in a little matter. He was tall and thin, and usually spoke in a slow way as though he found the whole of life slightly amusing. He didn't look

talent, special ability or skill
murderer, person who has murdered someone (see grammar, page 96)
routine, regular, ordinary
petty, of very little importance

amused now. His wife, Roz, was a *solid* girl in her late twenties. Present was also the faithful Mr Bernard, who has always acted as *solicitor* to the Timson family.

'They wouldn't let Tracy take even a doll. Not one of her Barbies. How do you think people could do that to a child?' Roz asked me when Mr Bernard had given a description of the details of the case. Her eyes were red from crying.

'*Nicking* your kid. That's what it's come to. Well, I'll allow us Timsons may have done a fair bit of *mischief* in our time. But no one in the family's ever done such a low thing, Mr Rumpole. People what* nick kids get boiling tea poured over their heads, when they're inside like.'

'Cary loves that girl, Mr Rumpole,' Roz told me. 'No matter what they say. You'll get Tracy back for us, won't you? She'll be that unhappy.'

'What's her crime, Mr Rumpole?' Cary asked. 'That's what Roz and I wants* to know. It's not as though she nicked things ever. Our Tracy is too young for any serious nicking.'

'Childhood itself seems a crime to some people.' It's a point that has often struck me.

'We can't seem to get any sense out of that Miss Jones.' Roz looked *helpless*.

'Jones?'

solid, firm and strongly made
solicitor, lawyer who prepares legal papers for a barrister, gives legal advice, and (in the lower courts only) speaks for his client
nick, (slang) to steal
mischief, action that causes troubles to others
*Cockney
*Cockney
helpless, needing the help of other people; not able to do anything for oneself

'Officer in charge of case. Tracy's social worker.'

'One of the "caring" people.' I was sure of it. 'All she'll say is that she's making further inquiries,' Mr Bernard told me. 'I've been talking to the solicitor for the Local Authority,' he reported, 'and their case is that Tracy Timson has been taking part in devil *worship* and *satanic rituals*.'

I will now give you an account of the filmed interview with Dominic Molloy which we finally saw at the *trial*. Before that, Mr Bernard had received a written copy of this *dramatic* scene. So, by bits and pieces, we realized what strange charges had been made against young Tracy. It began to look like a case which should not be decided at Crockthorpe Juvenile Court but in Spain in the darkest days of the *Inquisition*.

The scene was set in the headmistress's office in Stafford Cripps Junior. Mirabelle Jones, at her most *reassuring*, sat smiling on one side of the desk, while young Dominic Molloy sat on the other, full of self-importance.

'You remember the children wearing those terrible masks at school, do you, Dominic?' Mirabelle began.

'They frightened me!' Dominic *shuddered*.

worship, to pay honour to (a god); religious service
satanic, of Satan
ritual, particular set of fixed actions used in religious worship
trial, legal process in which a person is judged in a court of law
dramatic, exciting
Inquisition, court under the Roman Catholic Church for the discovery and punishment of persons considered to be against the church
reassure, to take away (a person's) doubts and fear
shudder, to tremble from fear

'I'm sure they did.' The social worker made a note, gave the camera – set up in a corner of the room – a little smile and then returned to the work in hand.

'Did you see who was leading those children?'

'In the end I did.' 5

'Who was it?'

'Trace.'

'Tracy Timson?'

'Yes.'

'Your mum said you went round to Tracy Timson's a few 10 times. After school, was that?'

'Yes. After school like.'

'And you said you went somewhere else. Where else, exactly?'

'Where they put people.' 15

'A churchyard. Was it a churchyard?' Mirabelle gave us a good example of a leading question. Dominic nodded and she made a note. 'The one in Crockthorpe Road? St Elphick's church?' Mirabelle suggested and Dominic nodded again. 'It was the churchyard. Was it dark?' 20 Dominic nodded so strongly that his whole body seemed to rock backwards and forwards and he was in danger of falling off his chair.

'After school and late. A month ago? So it was dark. Did a grown-up come with you? A man, perhaps. Did a 25 man come with you?'

'He said we was to play a game.' Dominic whispered.

'What sort of game?'

'He put something on his face.'

'A mask?' 30

'Red and *horns* on it.'

| *horn*, see picture, page 8

'A devil's mask.' Mirabelle was taking more notes.

'Is that right, Dominic? He wanted you to play at devils? This man did?'

'He said he was the Devil. Yes.'

'And what were you supposed to be?'

Dominic didn't answer that, but sat as if afraid to move.

'Perhaps you were the Devil's children?'

At this point Dominic's silence was more effective than any answer.

'Now, I want you to tell me, Dominic, when did you meet this man? At Tracy Timson's house? Is that where you met him?' More silence from Dominic, so Mirabelle tried again. 'Do you know who he was, Dominic?' At which Dominic nodded and looked around fearfully.

'Who was he, Dominic? You've been such a help to me so far. Can't you tell me who he was?'

'Tracy's dad.'

A few weeks after my conference with Tracy's parents I met Miss Liz Probert, my ex-pupil, when I blew into the clerk's room in Equity Court after a hard day's work. She had just picked up a *brief* and was looking at it with every sign of delight. Liz, the daughter of Red Ron Probert, Labour leader on the Crockthorpe Council, is the most *radical* member of our Chambers. I greeted her with, 'Soft you now! The fair *Mizz* Probert! What are you holding in your hand, old thing?' or words to that effect.

'What does it look like, Rumpole?'

brief, here, statement of a client's case drawn up for the information of his barrister
radical, who holds radical views, that is wanting great or extreme political or social changes
Mizz, Miss

'I'm afraid it looks like a brief.'

'Got it in one!' Mizz Liz was in a good mood that morning.

'Time marches on! My ex-pupil has begun to get briefs. What is it? Bad case of a missing dog?' 5

'A bit more serious than that. I'm for the Crockthorpe Local Authority, Rumpole.'

'I am filled with respect.' I didn't ask whether the presence of Red Ron on the Council had anything to do with her *extraordinary* luck, and Mizz Liz went on to tell 10 a familiar story. 'A little girl had to be taken into care. She was in terrible danger in the home. You know what it is – the father's got a criminal record. As a matter of fact, it's a name that might be familiar to you. Timson.'

'So they took away a Timson child because the father's 15 got a criminal record?' I asked.

'Not just that. Something rather awful was going on. Devil worship! The family were deeply into it. Quite seriously. It's a shocking case.'

'Is it really? Tell me, do you believe in the Devil?' 20

'Of course I don't, Rumpole. Don't be silly. Anyway that's hardly the point.'

'Isn't it? It interests me, though. You see, I'm likely to be against you in the Juvenile Court.'

'You, Rumpole! On the side of the Devil?' Mizz Probert 25 seemed shocked.

'Why not? They tell me he has the best lines.'

'Defending devil-worshippers, in a **children's** case! That's really not on, is it, Rumpole?'

'I really can't think of anyone I wouldn't defend. That's 30 what I believe in. I was just on my way to Pommeroy's.

| *extraordinary*, out of the ordinary, unusual

Mizz Liz, old thing, will you have a glass with me?'

'I really don't think we should be seen drinking together, now that I'm appearing for the Local Authority.'

5 'For the Local Authority, of course!' I gave her a respectful bow on leaving. 'A great power in the land! Even if they do sometimes get in the way of the joy of living.'

No sooner had I got to Pommeroy's Wine Bar and 10 started on my first glass when Claude Erskine-Brown came into view. Claude is married to Phillida Erskine-Brown, Q.C., both are respected members of our Chambers. 'An eight-year-old Timson has been locked up against her will, not in Eton College, but in the loving 15 care of the Crockthorpe Local Authority. The child is *suspected of* devil-worship. Can you believe it?' Claude was very excited.

'Well, I happen to be on the side of the devil-worshippers.'

20 'Is that your case, Rumpole?' Erskine-Brown looked deeply interested.

'Indeed, yes. And I have a strong *opponent*. None other than Mizz Liz Probert, with the full power of the Local Authority behind her. But I shall fight her with my sword 25 drawn.' And I left the bar holding high my umbrella. On my way out I heard a couple of young solicitors say, 'Funny old chap!'

Q.C., Queen's Counsel, title given to a barrister, see note, page 3
counsel, lawyer acting for someone in a court of law
suspected of, believed to have done (something wrong)
opponent, person who fights against someone or something

It was a time when everyone seemed busy *investigating* the devil-worshippers. Mirabelle Jones continued to make films for showing before the Juvenile Court and this time she interviewed Tracy Timson in a room, also with a video-camera, in the Children's Home.

Mirabelle arrived with some dolls. Not very beautiful but rather common ones, representing a Mum and Dad, *Grandpa* and *Grandma*. They looked like New England farm-workers. Tracy was ordered to play with this group. When, without any real interest in the matter, she managed to get Grandpa lying on top of Mum, Miss Jones kept her breath and made notes which she underlined heavily.

Later, Tracy was shown a book in which there was a picture of a devil with a long tail.

'You know who he is, don't you, Tracy?' Mirabelle was being particularly friendly as she asked this.

'No.'

'He's the Devil. You know about devils, don't you?' And she added, still smiling, 'You put on a devil's mask at school, didn't you, Tracy?'

'I might have done,' Tracy admitted.

'So what do you think of the devil, then?'

'He looks funny.' Tracy was smiling, which I thought was very brave of her, considering the situation.

'Funny?'

'He's got a tail. The tail's funny.'

'Who told you first about the Devil, Tracy?'

'I don't know,' the child answered, but Miss Jones was not to be put off so easily.

investigate, to make an official inquiry (into)
grandpa, *grandma*, grandfather, grandmother

'Oh, you must know. Did you hear about the Devil at home? Was that it? Did Dad tell you about the Devil?' Tracy shook her head. Mirabelle Jones tried again. 'Does that picture of the Devil remind you of anyone, Tracy?' 5 Still getting no answer, Mirabelle put a leading question, as was her way in these interviews. 'Do you think it looks like your dad at all?'

In search of an answer to Miss Jones's unanswered question, I asked Cary and Roz to come to my office 10 again. When they arrived I put the matter directly before them. At the mention of the Devil, Tracy's mother looked *puzzled*. 'The Devil? Tracy don't know nothing about the Devil.'*

'Of course not!' Cary said immediately. 'It's not as if we 15 went to church, Mr Rumpole.'

'You've never heard of such a suggestion before?' I looked hard at Tracy's father. 'The Devil. Satan. Are you saying the Timson family knows nothing of such matters? When they came that morning to get your Tracy, what 20 did you think was going on exactly?' I asked Cary.

'I thought they come about that shop that got done over, Wedges, down Gunston Avenue. They've had me down the *nick* time and time again about it.'

'And it wasn't you?'

25 'Straight up, Mr Rumpole. Would I lie to you?'

'It has been known, but I'll believe you. Do you know who did it?' I asked Cary.

to be puzzled, to be unable to understand the meaning (of something)
*Cockney
nick, (slang) prison or police-station

'No, Mr Rumpole. No, I won't *grass*. That I won't do. I've had enough trouble because they thought I had grassed on Gareth Molloy when he was sent down for the Tobler Road supermarket job.'

'The Timsons and the Molloys are deadly enemies. How could you know what they were up to?' 5

'My friend Barry Peacock was driving for them on that occasion. They thought I knew something and grassed to *Chief Inspector* Brush. Would I do a thing like that?'

'No, I don't suppose you would. So you thought the Old Bill were just there about the ordinary, lawful crime. You had no worries about Tracy?' 10

'She's a good girl, Mr Rumpole. Always has been,' Roz was quick to remind me.

'So where the devil do these ideas come from? Sorry, perhaps I shouldn't have said that ... You know Dominic Molloy told the social worker you taught a lot of children satanic rituals.' 15

'You ever believed a Molloy, have you, Mr Rumpole, in court or out of it?' Cary Timson had a good point there, but would the Juvenile Court trust me? 20

When our conference was over I showed the Timsons out and I thought I saw the face of Erskine-Brown in the open doorway at the end of the corridor. The door was shut as I noticed him. Twenty minutes later I received a visit from Samuel Ballard, Q.C., our so-salled Head of Chambers. I believe these events were connected. As soon as he got in, Ballard said, 'You've had them in here, Rumpole?' 25

'Had who in here, Ballard?' 30

'Those who worship the Evil One.'

grass, (slang) to give information of a crime to the police
chief inspector, police officer of higher rank

'You mean the Mr Justice Graves fan club? No, they haven't been near the place.'

'Rumpole! You know perfectly well who I mean.'

'Oh, yes. Of course. Lucifer, Beelzebub, Belial.* All present and correct. Grow up, Ballard! I am representing an eight-year-old child who's been torn away from her family and *banged up* without trial.'

'So you protect the devil-worshippers!' Ballard said.

'Those too. If necessary.'

'Rumpole. Every *decent* Chambers has to draw the line somewhere.'

'Does it?'

'There are certain cases, certain clients, even, we should not accept. There is something in this room which makes me feel uneasy.'

'Oh, I do so agree. Perhaps you'll be leaving shortly. And if you call again, don't forget the Holy Water!'

'I'm giving you a fair warning, Rumpole. I expect you to think it over.' At which our leader made for the door.

When the man had gone and I was left alone to wonder exactly what *devilment* Cary Timson had been up to.

I had a reason, which I'll explain at a proper moment, to telephone a Miss Tatiana Fern and I didn't wish to do so with Hilda's knowledge. As the lady in question left her house early, I called when I thought She was still asleep. I now believe Hilda was listening in on the bedroom telephone, although she lay with her eyes closed when I

*names given to the Evil One in various religions
bang up, (slang) lock up
decent, that acts according to good taste and moral standards
devilment, strange or evil happenings; way of acting that causes harm

came back to bed. Later I discovered that when Hilda went off to shop in Harrods she saw me coming out of Knightsbridge tube station, a place far removed from the Temple and the Old Bailey*. She tracked me to a house in Mowbray Crescent which she saw me enter when the front door was opened by Tatiana Fern. So it came about that She met Marigold, Mr Justice Featherstone's wife, and together they formed the opinion that Rumpole was up to no good whatsoever.

Of course, she didn't talk to me openly about this, but when I was about to leave one morning she said darkly, 'Enjoy your lunch-hour!'

'What did you say?'

'I said, "I hope you enjoy you lunch-hour," Rumpole.'

'Well, I probably shall. It's Thursday. Meat *pie* day at the pub in Ludgate Circus. I shall look forward to that.'

'And a few other little *treats* besides, I should imagine.'

Hilda was engaged in reading her newspaper again when I left her. I knew then that, no matter what explanation I had given, She Who Must Be Obeyed had come to believe that I was up to something devilish.

pie

It is a strange fact that this was the first time in my life that I was called upon to perform in a Juvenile Court. It was, as I was soon to discover, a place in which the law as we know and sometimes love it had very little place.

*London Central Criminal Court
treat, here, something that gives great pleasure

Tracy's three judges, with a large motherly-looking *magistrate* as *chairwoman*, sat with their *clerk* in a cold room in Crockthorpe's courthouse. The defence team, Rumpole and the faithful Bernard, together with the 5 *prosecutor* Mizz Liz Probert, and a person from the Council solicitor's office, sat at another long table opposite the justices. Miss Mirabelle Jones sat comfortably in the witness chair, armed with a pile of papers, and a large televison set was playing that hit video, the 10 inverview with Dominic Molloy.

We had got to the familiar line of questioning which started with Mirabelle asking: 'He wanted you to play at devils? This man did?'

'He said he was the Devil. Yes,' the picture of the boy 15 Dominic alleged.

'He was to be the Devil. And what were you supposed to be? Perhaps you were the Devil's children?'

At which point Rumpole ruined the show by objecting and pointing out that this was a leading question. 'It and 20 the answer are entirely *inadmissible*, as your clerk will no doubt tell you.' And I added in a loud whisper to Bernard, 'If he knows his business.'

'Mr Rumpole' – the chairwoman gave me her most motherly smile – 'Miss Mirabelle Jones is an extremely 25 experienced social worker. We think we can trust her to put her questions in the proper manner.'

magistrate, official who has the power to judge cases in the lowest courts of law, esp a police-court
chairman, -person, -woman, person who takes charge of or directs a meeting
clerk, here, lawyer working for the Council
prosecutor, lawyer who brings a criminal charge against someone in a court of law
inadmissible, not to be allowed

'I was trying to point out that on this occasion she put her question in an entirely *improper* way,' I told her, 'Madam.'

'My *Bench* will see the film out to the end, Mr Rumpole. You'll have a chance to make any points later.' 5
The clerk gave his decision in a manner which caused me to whisper to Mr Bernard, 'Her Master's Voice.' I hope they all heard, but to make myself clear I said to Madam Chair, 'My point is that you shouldn't be seeing this film at all.' 10

'We are going to continue with it now, Mr Rumpole.' The *learned* clerk switched on the video again. Miss Jones appeared to say, 'Now I want you to tell me, Dominic, when did you meet this man? At Tracy Timson's house? Is that where you met him?' 15

'It's a leading question!' I said in a loud voice. But the interview continued and Mirabelle asked, 'Do you know who he was?' And on the video Dominic nodded.

'Who was he?' Mirabelle asked and Dominic replied, 'Tracy's dad.' 20

As the video was switched off, I was on my feet again. 'You're not going to allow this as *evidence*?' I couldn't believe it. 'Pure *hearsay*!. What a child who isn't called as a witness said to Miss Jones here, a child we've had no opportunity of *cross-examining* said, is nothing but 25

improper, not proper, not correct
Bench, (law) area where the judge sits; judges generally
learned, having great learning, here, way of addressing a fellow laywer in court
evidence, here, information that helps to prove something in a court of law
hearsay, something that you have been told about, but which you cannot be certain is true because you have not seen or experienced it for yourself
cross-examine, here, to question (a witness for the other side)

hearsay. Absolutely worthless.'

'Madam chairwoman.' Mizz Liz Probert rose politely beside me.

'Yes, Miss Probert.' Liz got an even more motherly smile; she was the favourite child and Rumpole the black sheep of the family.

'Mr Rumpole is used to practising at the Old Bailey –'

'And has become familiar with the law of evidence,' I added.

'And of course this court is not bound by rules of evidence. Where the welfare of a child is concerned, you're not tied down by a lot of legal *quibbles* about hearsay.'

'Quibbles, Mizz Probert? Did I hear you say quibbles?' I shouted.

'You are free,' Liz told the judges, 'with the able *assistance* of Miss Mirabelle Jones, to get at the truth of this matter.'

'Mr Rumpole,' the clerk of the court added, 'I don't think my Bench wants to waste time on a legal argument.'

'Do they not? Indeed!' No one was going to stop me now. 'So does it come to this? Down at the Old Bailey, that place civilization hasn't reached yet, no villain can be sent to prison as a result of a leading question, or what a child said to a social worker and wasn't even cross-examined. But little Tracy Timson, eight years old, can be banged up for God knows how long, taken from the family that loves her, without the protection the law affords to a bank robber! Is that what Mizz Liz Probert is

quibble, unimportant argument
assistance, help

telling the court? And which seems to find favour in the so-called legal mind of the court official?'

Even as I spoke the clerk was whispering to Madam Chair. 'Mr Rumpole, my Bench would like to get on with the evidence. Speeches will come later,' the chairwoman handed down her clerk's decision.

'They will, Madam. They most certainly will,' I promised. And then, as I sat down, Liz dared to teach me my business. 'Let me give you a tip, Rumpole,' she whispered. 'I should keep off the law if I were you. They don't like it around here.'

The chairwoman now addressed Mirabelle with a smile. 'Miss Jones,' she said in a sweet voice, 'we are very pleased with the way you have gone into this difficult case for the Local Authority. And we've seen the interview you carried out with Tracy on the video film. Was there anything about that interview which you thought especially important?'

'It was when I showed her the picture of the Devil,' Mirabelle answered. 'She wasn't frightened at all. In fact she laughed. I thought … '

'Is there any point in my telling you that what this witness thought isn't evidence?' I sent up a cry of *protest*.

'Carry on, Miss Jones. If you'd be so kind.'

'I thought it was because it reminded her of someone she knew pretty well. Someone like Dad.' Mirabelle said.

'Someone like Dad. Yes.' Our Chair was now making a careful note, likely to ruin Tracy's hopes of liberty.

'Have you any questions, Mr Rumpole?'

So I rose to cross-examine. It's not easy to attack a good-looking young woman from one of the caring professions.

| *protest*, strong statement of being against something

But this Mirabelle Jones was, so far as my case was concerned, a killer. I decided to go in with all guns firing. 'Miss Jones,' I began, 'you are, I take it, against *cruelty* to children?'

5 'Of course. That goes without saying.'

'Does it? Can you think of a more cruel act, to a little child, than coming early in the morning with the Old Bill and taking it away from its mother and father, without even a Barbara doll for *consolation*?'

10 'Barbie doll, Mr Rumpole,' Roz whispered.

'What?'

'It's a Barbie doll, Mrs Timson says,' Mr Bernard said.

'Very well, Barbie doll.' And I returned to the attack on Mirabelle. 'Without that, or a single toy?'

15 'We don't want the children to be reminded of home.'

'You wanted Tracy only to think about your silly idea of devil-worship!' I said.

'It wasn't a silly idea, Mr Rumpole, and I had to act quickly. Tracy had to be taken away from the presence of 20 evil.'

'Evil? What do you mean by that exactly?' The witness didn't answer, being at a loss for a proper explanation, and Mizz Liz Probert rose to save her. 'You ought to know, Mr Rumpole. Haven't you had plenty of experience of 25 that down at the Old Bailey?'

'Oh, well played, Mizz Probert! Your days as a pupil are over. Now, Miss Mirabelle Jones' – I turned to my real opponent – 'let's come down to what, at the Old Bailey, we call hard facts. You know that my client, Mr Cary

cruelty, the act of being *cruel*, pleased at causing pain
consolation, something which makes loss or pain more easy to bear

Timson, is a small-time thief and villain?'

'I have given the Bench the list of Dad's criminal *convictions*, yes.'

'It's not the sort of record, is it, Mr Rumpole, that you might expect a good father to have?' The Chair smiled as she invited me to agree, but I didn't. 'Oh, I don't know,' I said. ' Are only the most *law-abiding* citizens meant to have children? If we took away the children from all crooks and villains this Local Authority would run out of children's homes to bang them up in.'

'Speeches come later, Mr Rumpole.' The clerk could keep silent no longer.

'They will,' I promised him. 'Cary Timson is a *humble* member of the Clan Timson, that vast family of South London villains. Now, remind us of the name of that *imaginative* little boy you interviewed on television.'

'Dominic Molloy.' Mirabelle knew it by heart. 'Molloy, yes. And, as we've been told so often, you are an extremely experienced social worker.'

'I think so.'

'With a good knowledge of the social life in this part of South London?'

'I get to know a good deal. Yes, of course I do.'

'Of course. So it will come as no surprise to you if I suggest that the Molloys are a large family of villains of a slightly more dangerous nature than the Timsons.'

'I don't know that. But if you say so ... '

'Oh, I do say so. Did you meet Dominic's mother, Mrs

conviction, here, sentence for a crime
law-abiding, obeying the law
humble, unimportant; having a low position in society
imaginative, having the ability of forming pictures in the mind, often of something which is not true or does not exist

Peggy Molloy?'

'Oh, yes. I had a good talk with Mum. Over a *cuppa*.' The Bench and Mirabelle exchanged smiles.

'And over a cuppa did she tell you that her husband was in Wandsworth prison as a result of the Tobler Road supermarket affair?'

'Mr Rumpole. My Bench is wondering if this is entirely *relevant*.' The clerk had been whispering to the Chair and handed the words down from on high.

'Then let your Bench keep quiet and listen,' I told him. 'It'll soon find out. So what's the answer, Miss Jones? Did you know that?'

'I didn't know that Dominic's father was in prison.' Miss Jones said lightly.

'And that he suspected Tracy's dad, as you would call him, of having been the police informer who put him there?'

'Did he?' The witness seemed to find all this talk of *adult* crime somewhat uninteresting.

'Oh, yes. And I shall be calling hearsay evidence to prove it. Miss Jones, are you telling this Bench that you, an experienced social worker, didn't care to find out about the deep hate that exists between the Molloys and the Timsons, stretching back to the dark days when Crockthorpe was a village and the local villains *swung* at the crossroads?'

'I have nothing about that in my *file*,' Mirabelle told us,

cuppa, (slang) cup of tea
relevant, having to do with what is being spoken about
adult, grown-up
swung, here, were hanged
file, any collection of papers kept together, having to do with a certain case or person

as though that made all such evidence completely unimportant.

'Nothing in your file. And your file hasn't considered the possibility that young Dominic Molloy has put an *innocent* little girl of a rival family "*in the frame*", as we call 5
it down at the Old Bailey?'

'Oh, I hardly believe that.'

'You don't, Miss Jones, you who believe in devil-worship?'

'I believe in evil influences on children.' Mirabelle 10
chose her words carefully. 'Yes.'

'Then let's just examine that. It all began when a number of children appeared in the playground of Crockthorpe Junior wearing masks?'

'Devil's masks. Yes.' 15

'Yet the only one you took into so-called care was Tracy Timson?'

'She was the leader. I discovered that Tracy had brought the masks to school in the bag with her lunch and her reading books.' 20

'Did you ask her where she got them from?'

'I did. Of course, she wouldn't tell me.' Mirabelle smiled and I knew a possible reason for Tracy's silence. Even if Cary Timson had been engaged in satanic rituals his daughter would never have grassed on him. 'I *assumed* 25
it was from her father.' Mirabelle went on.

'Miss Mirabelle Jones. Let's hope that at some point we'll get to a little *reliable* evidence, and that this case

innocent, who has done nothing wrong
put someone "in the frame", make others believe that an innocent person has taken part in a crime
assume, to take as true without being certain
reliable, able to be trusted or counted on

doesn't depend entirely on your *assumptions*.'

The lunchbreak came none too soon and Mr Bernard and I went in search of a watering-hole. The Jolly Grocer was to Pommeroy's Wine Bar what the Crockthorpe Court was to the Old Bailey. It was a large, dull pub. Pommeroy's red wine may be at the bottom end of the market, but I was afraid that The Jolly Grocer's red would be even worse. After a couple of bottles of Guinness and a meat pie we started the short walk back to the Crockthorpe courthouse.

On the way I let Bernard know my view of the case so far. 'It's all very well to *accuse* the deeply caring Miss Mirabelle Jones of guessing,' I told him, 'but we've got to tell the old darlings on the bench where the hell the masks came from.'

'Our client, Mr Cary Timson ... '

'You mean "Dad"?'

'Yes. He *denies* all knowledge.'

'Does he?' And then, quite suddenly, I stopped. I found myself outside a shop called Wedges Carnival and Novelty Stores*. The window was full of games, *fancy-dress*, hats, Father Christmas *costumes*, masks and other things for parties and general merrymaking. It was while I was staring at these goods that I said to Mr Bernard, in the tone of someone watching the skies when a new star

assumption, the act of assuming
accuse, to charge with wrong-doing; to blame
deny, to declare not to be true; to say "no" to
*shop that sells masks and *fancy-dress* etc.
fancy-dress, clothes representing a particular character, nationality, period or the like
costume, clothes

comes into sight, 'Well, he would, wouldn't he? The honour of the Timsons.'

'What do you mean, Mr Rumpole?'

'What's the name of this street? Is it by any chance . . . ?'

It was. 'Gunston Avenue,' Mr Bernard said, looking up a street sign.

'Who robbed Wedges?' We had arrived back at the courthouse with ten minutes in hand and I found Cary Timson smoking a last cigarette outside the main entrance. His wife was with him and I lost no time in asking the important question.

'Mr Rumpole' – Tracy's dad looked round and said in a low voice – 'you know I can't –'

'Grass? The rules of honour of the Timsons? Well, let me tell you, Cary. There's something even more important than the honour of the Timsons.'

'I don't know it, then.'

'Oh, yes, you do. You know perfectly well. Is your much-loved Tracy less important than honour among thieves?' I asked them both. Roz gave her husband a determined look. I knew then what the answer to my question would have to be.

The afternoon dragged on without any new events, and although Cary had told me what I needed to know he had not yet permitted me to use the information. The extended Timson family would have to be *consulted*. When the day's work was done I took the tube back to the Temple and went at once to Pommeroy's for a glass of Château Fleet Street.

That night important events were taking place in my

1 *consult*, to ask for advice or information

client's home in Morrison Close, Crockthorpe. Numerous Timsons were gathered in the front room. Cary's Uncle Fred, the head of the family, was there, as was Uncle Dennis, who should long ago have *retired*
5 from a life of crime to his holiday home on the Costa del Sol. Roz gave me a full account of what was said. After a general family discussion and exchange of news, Uncle Fred gave his opinion of the Wedges job. 'Bloody joke shop. I always said it was a bad idea, robbing a joke shop.'
10 'There was always money left overnight. Our information told us that. And we could get through the backdoor easily,' Uncle Dennis explained.

'What did you want to leave the stuff round my place for?' Cary was naturally sorry that the *booty* had included
15 a box of satanic masks and that they had been left in his garage where it had been easy for Tracy to find them. 'You should have known how dangerous them things were, what with young kids and social workers about.'*

'Well, Fred's place was under *surveillance*,' Uncle
20 Dennis explained. 'As was mine. And seeing that you and Roz was* away on Monday ... And knowing where you kept the garage key ... '

'Lucky the Bill never thought of looking there,' Cary pointed out.
25 'I meant to come back for the stuff some time. It slipped my memory, quite honestly. It didn't seem very important. I'm sorry.'

retire, to give up work because of old age
booty, goods taken from an enemy by force, here, that which is stolen
*Cockney
surveillance, close watch or guard
*Cockney

'Well, it was important for our Tracy.'

'I know, Roz. Sorry about that.'

'Look, Den,' Cary started. 'We're not asking you to put your hands up to Chief Inspector Brush ... '

'Yes, we are, Cary.' Roz was deadly serious. 'That's just what we're asking. You got to do it for our Tracy.' 5

'Hang about a bit,' Uncle Dennis said. 'Who says we got to?'

And then Roz told him, 'Mr Rumpole.'

So the next morning Dennis Timson gave evidence in 10 the Juvenile Court. 'I was after the money, really,' Dennis told the Bench. 'But I suppose I got a bit *greedy*, like. I just put a few of those boxes in the back of the car. Then I didn't want to take them round to my place, so I left them in Cary's garage.' 15

'Why did you do that?' I asked.

'Well, young Cary didn't have anything to do with the Wedges job, so I thought they'd be safe enough there. Of course, I was under great pressure of work at that time, and it slipped my mind to tell Cary and Roz about it.' 20

'Did you see what was in any of those cases?'

'I had a little look-in. Seemed like a lot of carnival masks. That sort of stuff.'

'So young Tracy getting hold of the devil's masks was just the usual Timson *cock-up*, was it?' 25

'What did you say, Mr Rumpole?' The chairwoman wasn't quite sure she could believe her ears.

'The usual stock-up, for Christmas, Madam Chair,' I explained. 'Oh, one more thing, Mr Dennis Timson. Do you know why young Dominic Molloy has accused Tracy 30

greedy, having a (too) great desire for something
cock-up, (slang) failure of success because things are done badly

and her father of satanic rituals in a churchyard?'

'Course I do.' Uncle Den had no doubt. 'Peggy Molloy told Barry Peacock's wife and Barry's wife told my Doreen down at the Needle Arms last Thursday.'

5 'We can't possibly have this evidence!' Liz Probert rose to object. Perhaps she'd caught the habit from me.

'Oh, really, Miss Probert? And why ever not?'

'What Barry's wife told Mrs Timson is pure hearsay.' Mizz Probert was certain of it.

10 'Of course it is.' And I gave her back her own argument. 'And pure hearsay is totally *acceptable* in the Juvenile Court. Where the interest of the child is concerned we are not bound by legal quibbles. I agree, Madam Chair, with every word which has fallen from your respected and 15 highly learned clerk. Now then, Mr Timson, what did you hear exactly?'

'Gareth thought Cary had grassed on him over the Tobler Road supermarket job. So they got young Dominic to put the frame round Tracy and her dad.'

20 'So what you are telling us, Mr Timson, is that this little boy's evidence was a pure invention.' At last Madam Chair seemed to have got the message. Uncle Dennis gave her the most charming and friendliest of smiles as he said, 'Well, you can't trust the Molloys, can 25 you, my Lady? Everyone knows they're a right family of villains.'

There comes a time in many cases when the wind changes. Uncle Dennis's evidence changed the weather, and after it I noticed that Madam Chair no longer 30 returned Miss Mirabelle Jones's smile. Mizz Probert's final address was listened to in dead silence and I was

| *acceptable*, that can be accepted

surprised to hear a clear "thank you" from the Bench as I sat down. After a short period of *retirement* the powers that were to shape young Tracy Timson's future declared that they were not satisfied by the evidence of any satanic rituals and she was, therefore, to be *released*. Before this judgement was over, the tears which Roz had fought to control since that terrible morning were released and, at her moment of joy, she cried helplessly.

I got into Mr Bernard's car and followed the Timson Cortina to the Children's Home. We waited until we saw the mother and father come out from the building, each holding one of their daughter's hands. As they came down the steps to the street they swung her in the air

retirement, here, place away from public notice
release, set free

between them, and when they got into the car they were laughing. Miss Mirabelle Jones, who had brought the order for release, stood in the doorway of the Lilacs and watched without expression, and then Tracy's legal team drove away to do other cases with less happy results.

When I got home, after a glass at Pommeroy's Wine Bar in honour of the occasion, Hilda was not in the best of *moods*. When I brought her the good news, all She said was, 'You seem full of yourself, Rumpole. Been having a good time, have you?'

'A great time! Managed to get young Tracy Timson away from the caring society and back to her family. And I'll be getting another brief defending Dennis Timson on a charge of stealing from Wedges Carnival Shop. Well, I expect I'll think of something.'

'You never wanted to be a judge, did you Rumpole,' Hilda said somewhat darkly.

'Judging people? Passing sentences on to them? No, that's not my line, exactly. Anyway, judges are meant to keep quiet in court.'

'And they're much more *restricted*, aren't they?' It may have sounded an innocent question on a matter of general interest, but her voice sounded threatening.

'Restricted?' I repeated, playing for time.

'Sitting in court all day, in the public eye and having to behave well. They have far less time than you have for other activities ... '

'Activities, Hilda?'

'Oh, yes. Perhaps it's about time we really talked for

mood, state of mind
restrict, to keep (a person) within a certain limit

once, Rumpole. Is there something that you feel you ought to tell me?'

'Well. Yes, Hilda. Yes. As a matter of fact there is.' I had in fact done something which I felt was strangely difficult to mention. 5

'Rumpole! How could you?'

'But I did it at an *enormous* expense.'

'You had to pay!' Hilda was angry.

'Well, they don't give these things away for nothing.'

'I imagine not!' 10

'One hundred *smackers*. But it **is** your birthday next week.'

'Rumpole! I can't think what my birthday's got to do with it.' At least I had managed to puzzle her a little.

'Everything, Hilda. I've just bought us two tickets for 15 the Scales of Justice Ball. Now, what was it **you** wanted to talk about?'

'Well,' she said, 'not at the moment. Perhaps some other time.'

Matters were not altogether settled when we found 20 ourselves at a table by the dance floor in the Savoy Hotel in the company of Sam Ballard and his wife, Marguerite. Also present were Marigold Featherstone, wife of a judge, Claude Erskine-Brown and Liz Probert with her partner and fellow member of 3 Equity Court, young Dave Inch- 25 cape.

'Too bad Guthrie's sitting at Newcastle!' Claude said to Marigold Featherstone, referring to her husband. 'Philly's in Swansea on a murder case.'

'Never mind, Claude,' Marguerite Ballard said, 'I'll 30 dance with you.'

enormous, very large
smacker, (slang) pound (money)

'Oh, yes, Erskine-Brown' – her husband was smiling – 'you are permitted to shake foot with my wife.'

'Oh, well. Yes. Thank you very much.'

'Now, as Head of Chambers,' Ballard continued, 'I think I should lead my wife out on to the floor.'

'No. No, Ballard. With all due respect' – I rose to my feet – 'as the longest-serving Chambers wife, She that is Mrs Rumpole should be led out first. Care for a dance, Hilda?'

'Rumpole! Are you sure you can manage it?' Hilda was *astonished*.

'I have all confidence, thank you.' And I immediately put one hand around her *waist*, seized her hand with the other, and led her out on to the dancing floor. There I turned her around in time to the music and even did a little fancy footwork as we passed a table full of solicitors. 'You're *chasséing*, Rumpole!' She was astonished.

'Oh, yes. I do that quite a lot nowadays.'

'Wherever did you learn?'

'To be quite honest with you ... '

'If that is possible.' She had not been completely won over.

'From a Miss Tatiana Fern. I looked her up in the Yellow Pages.* One-time Southern Counties Ballroom Champion. I took a few lessons.'

'Where did you take lessons?'

'Place called Mowbray Crescent.'

'Somewhere off Sloane Street?'

astonished, greatly surprised
chassé, to make a certain step in dancing
*in the telephone book

Rumpole has his hand around her waist

'Hilda! You knew?'

'Oh, don't ever think you can do anything I don't know about.' At which point the Ballards passed us, not dancing perfectly well together. 'You're really quite *nippy* on your feet, Rumpole. Marguerite Ballard's looking absolutely green with *envy*.' And then she actually smiled at me. 'You are an old devil, Rumpole!' she said.

nippy, quick-moving
envy, feeling of anger at other people's good fortune or success

Rumpole and the *Soothsayer*

However forward-looking we may all think we are, man is far more interested in his past than in his future. Down at the Bailey we spend days and weeks digging into the past, trying to discover exactly who it was who was seen outside the Eldorado Building Society in Surbiton on the day the Molloys did it over, or which exact words Tony Timson used in the police car when he admitted having broken into the Streatham Video Centre. But when it comes to the future we use one short sentence like, "You will go to prison for five years."

The future is a closed book which few people care to open. The exception to this rule was a client of mine, a somewhat unusual person called Roderick Arengo-Smythe, whose eyes were firmly fixed on the time ahead. The future was a subject on which he claimed to have a good deal of inside information, given to him by friends among dead people.

Arengo-Smythe didn't burst into my life in the way some clients do, as a result of a *robbery* or sudden death. He arrived much more quietly, as, I suppose, a man would who spent such a lot of time whispering to the *defunct*. I first came in touch with Arengo-Smythe in an indirect manner when one day I went into the clerk's room. Here I discovered *Soapy* Sam Ballard, Q.C., the man who, by

soothsayer, someone who can tell what is going to happen in the future. "Sooth" is an old word meaning "truth".
robbery, the act of robbing
defunct, dead person
soapy, like soap; (of person or his manners or talk) making a false show of sympathy or willingness, etc.

the workings of blind fate, became the Head of our Chambers, calling off the arrangements for some much-needed repairs to our downstairs *loo* set for December 14th of that year.

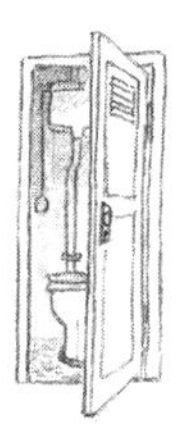

loo

'We've had all this trouble arranging the workmen, sir. Why does it have to be put off?' Henry, our clerk, protested.

Considering the downstairs loo now looks rather like the black hole of Calcutta in a poor state of repair, I agreed with Henry and said, 'Why not get on with it?'

'Not on the 14th of December,' Soapy Sam Ballard was very firm. 'I can't take the *responsibility* for that.'

'What on earth is wrong with the 14th of December?'

'No time to explain. I've got a tax case starting before Mr Justice Graves. And,' he added darkly as he left, 'why don't you ask your wife?'

After a quick thought, by no means new, that our Head of Chambers no longer was in his right mind, I forgot our strange conversation. That evening Hilda and I sat in our living room in Gloucester Road. I was defending Ronnie Timson at the time on matters arising out of the fight in the Needle Arms, Stockwell. We were half-way through

loo, lavatory, see picture above
responsibility, the state of having important duties so that one must take the blame if something goes wrong

the trial. Should I put Ronnie into the witness-box the next day to deny all charges?

What's the matter, Rumpole? *Wool-gathering*?' She Who Must Be Obeyed demanded my attention.

5 'No. No, of course not. The problem is, if I call Ronnie Timson to give evidence tomorrow he'll probably *convict* himself out of his own mouth, and if I don't the *jury*'ll think he's guilty anyway.'

'Don't you know what sort of witness Ronnie is going to 10 make?'

'Not exactly. I can't see into the future.'

'Well then, you should ring Marguerite Ballard.'

'Mrs Soapy Sam? Has she got some sort of *crystal ball*?'

'Not that. She's got a little man who can tell her about 15 the future.' She said it as though Mrs Ballard had rather a clever dressmaker round the corner. 'He's a fellow called Arengo-Smythe. It seems she goes to him for readings.'

'The works of Dickens?'

'No. The future. And she's taken Sam to him once or 20 twice.'

'Why? Is Ballard particularly interested in the future?'

'Of course. Since Judge Mathias died Sam's been hoping for a job on the High Court Bench.'

'And does Arengo-Smythe tell him when he's going to 25 get his bottom on the High Court Bench?'

'Marguerite didn't tell me that. But she did tell me that

wool-gathering, day-dreaming
convict, to find *guilty* of a crime
guilty, having done something wrong, here in breaking the law
jury, group of usually 12 people who hear evidence in court and must decide whether or not a prisoner is guilty
crystal ball, kind of glass ball in which some people believe they can see the future

Sam was terribly worried about something else he said.'
'What was that?'
'That there was a great black cloud over the 14th of December.'
And, as she said that, I began to understand. 5

One of the best-known facts about the world is that it is extremely small. So it came as no particular surprise to me to be told by Henry that my old friend Mr Bernard, the faithful solicitor who *goes out into the highways and byways* and brings me back criminal work, was coming 10 with a new client, a certain Roderick Arengo-Smythe, who was about to face trial at the Old Bailey. So I was to have the honour of meeting Sam Ballard's soothsayer.
Arengo-Smythe turned out to be a large and rather fat man. It was difficult to tell his age. His face was without 15 any colours and his hands were large and soft. This was the customer to whom it was my clear duty to put the charge of *fraud* and false *deception*.
'Mr Rumpole!' My client protested. 'Do you honestly think my spirit people would do something so low?' 20
'Well. Some of them might, I suppose. I mean, there must be quite a few villains among dead people.'
'They may be there, Mr Rumpole. But White *Owl* would spot them a mile away. He would never allow a bad person in my front room.' 25
'Even dead ones?'

go out into the highways and byways, to search high and low, to search everywhere
fraud, dishonest (not honest) dealings
deception, tricks; acts to make people believe what is not true
owl, see picture, page 51. Here name given to an Indian chief

'Particularly dead ones.'

'Just remind me . . . ' I searched through the open brief on my desk. 'Who is White Owl?'

'An ancient chief of the Sioux Indians, Mr Rumpole.'

5 Mr Bernard, my *instructing* solicitor, was used to

instruct, of solicitor, to give information to (counsel); to arrange to employ (a barrister) for a case

owl

repeating impossible defences in a *dead-pan* manner. 'He *copped it*, it seems, at the battle of Little Big Horn.'

'Not copped it, Mr Bernard, if you don't mind. The spirit people do not cop it. They pass over.'

'What is alleged is a perfectly simple *con-trick*.' I brought the meeting back to reality. 'You charged your customers no less than £50 a sitting.'

'Making the spirit people appear can make you very tired.'

'You told your customers that they were hearing the voice of White Owl. You said he could *foretell* the future?'

'All the spirit people can, Mr Rumpole. You'll be able to as well, when you've passed over.'

'Really? I can't wait. It's further suggested' – I was reading from the *Prosecution* statements – 'that Woman Police Constable Battley attended the *seance* as a

dead-pan, showing no feelings at all; looking serious without actually being it
cop it,(slang) to die
con-trick, confidence trick, trick to gain a person's trust (confidence) and then make him hand over money
foretell, to tell (about something) before it has happened
prosecution, the person or group of people who are concerned with bringing a criminal charge against someone in court
seance, meeting of people trying to receive messages from the spirits of the dead

member of the public. White Owl finally came through, after a good deal of delay.'

'White Owl can be very difficult on occasions, Mr Rumpole. He doesn't always want to come when he's sent 5 for.'

'Later she left the room saying she had to go to the lavatory. She went into the next room and discovered your sister Harriet holding a *microphone*. She then immediately asked for help from Detective *Sergeant* 10 Webster, who was waiting outside the front door, armed with a *search-warrant*. On entering your flat he found the microphone connected to a speaker taped under the table where your seance was going on.'

'Are you suggesting that my sister and I were *cheating*, 15 Mr Rumpole? Be quiet now, White Owl . . . ..' He said this to an unseen presence near his left shoulder. 'Don't break in when I'm trying to talk to Mr Rumpole. White Owl is getting a little angry, sir. He feels this case is questioning his honour.'

20 'Don't worry about White Owl. It's you, Mr Arengo-Smythe, they might put to prison. Was your sister Harriet connected to your living-room?'

'Yes, of course. She put that up so that we could talk when we were in different rooms.'

25 'Well now, what's your defence, Mr Arengo-Smythe?'

Understandably my client was at a loss for an answer. Then he said, 'You know Mr Samuel Ballard, don't you? He knows I'm not cheating.'

'That may not be enough to prove you're innocent.'

sergeant, police officer of the rank next above constable
search-warrent, legal paper which permits the police to search a house
cheat, to act in a way which is not honest to gain profit

And then I looked at him and I was curious to know. 'What exactly did you tell my Head of Chambers?'

'I told him what White Owl had seen when he came for a sitting with his wife.'

'And what was that?' 5

'A terrible black cloud hanging over the 14th of December. A day of extraordinary danger. What will you be doing on that precise date, Mr Rumpole?'

'Defending you down the Old Bailey!' I tried to say it as cheerfully as possible. 'By the way, when you're next 10 talking to White Owl, ask him to have a few words with the *late* Sir Edward Marshall-Hall. You'll need a very

| *late*, here, dead

clever defence to save you, old darling.'

As I walked down Fleet Street to Ludgate Circus to start, with very little hope of success, the case of *R. v.* Arengo-Smythe, I happened to catch up with Soapy Sam. He was on his way to one of his tax cases. I told the man I was defending his soothsayer.

'I know you are, Rumpole. I told him to see you. Both Marguerite and I think he's a very clever man. He really has the power of seeing into the future. You'll get him off, won't you?'

'Perhaps. If the judge and the jury have all passed over. He gets on extremely well with the dead. Oh, I forgot. He no doubt brought you news of great joy about your future as Mr Justice Ballard, the *terror* of the Queen's Bench.'

'He told me something in confidence, Rumpole. That was why I didn't think it proper to act for him myself.'

'Didn't he also tell you to *beware* of the 14th of December?'

'He did say he saw a black cloud hanging over that date, yes. That's why I thought it unwise to get the workmen into Chambers.'

Before entering the courtroom, I looked at the date on the Old Bailey notice-board. It was the 13th of December and our case was set down for two days.

Our Trial Judge was Mr Justice Teasdale: a small, highly

R., *Reigning Rex/Regina* (Latin for King/Queen) meaning the King or Queen as head of State *v. (versus)* against the accused, here Mr Arengo-Smythe
terror, here, someone who makes you very afraid
beware!, be careful!

opinionated person who was unmarried and lived in Surbiton with a Persian cat. The trial, dealing as it did with messages from the dead, seemed to make him nervous. He clearly wanted a simple and scientific explanation for Arengo-Smythe's alleged gift of seeing 5
into the future.

He was therefore greatly satisfied with the police evidence, and the description of the wire which stretched from a microphone in one room to the little speaker taped under the table next door. Sister Harriet, 10
who was found with the microphone, was not able to appear in court, having had a nervous breakdown before the trial. According to the doctor she was quite unfit to give evidence. However, the Woman Police Constable told us what she had seen and Detective Sergeant 15
Webster produced a microphone and a speaker connected by yards of dark wire.

'Did you take this *device* from my client's flat straight to the police station?' I asked the Detective Sergeant, more to kill time than because I had hit upon any particular 20
line of defence.

'Yes, sir, I did.'

'Just let me look at it, will you?'

The *exhibit* was brought to me in a plastic bag. I took the microphone out and looked at it, trying to look as if 25
I knew something about sound systems. I unrolled the black wire and started to follow it to its connection with the small speaker. And then I saw something which

opinionated, having very strong opinions which one is not willing to change
device, instrument made for a certain purpose
exhibit, (law) object produced in court as part of the evidence

seemed to offer Arengo-Smythe an unexpected escape from his troubles.

The wire divided at the speaker. It looked old and *rusted* and only one *strand* was connected. Without any knowledge of science even I knew that this was a serious fault. When the device was handed round the jury, among which were several Do-It-Yourself people, it was clear to everyone that on the night of the visit of W.P.C. Battley, the date of the charge against my client, the hotline to Harriet Arengo-Smythe couldn't possibly have been working.

'The device was out of order. Well, of course, I knew that. It hadn't worked for years.' Arengo-Smythe was in the witnessbox answering my questions.

'Did your sister know it too?'

'Oh, no. I let her carry on. She thought she was helping the spirits come through, you see. She'd done that since we started our work with the *occult*. That was before we charged for sittings, of course.'

'So when the Woman Police Constable came to your seance, there was no voice coming down the wire?'

'Certainly not.'

'Then where was it coming from?' the Judge asked rather worried.

My client, his large head turned as he looked over his shoulder, carried on a whispering conversation with someone unseen.

rusted, covered with *rust*, that is the substance which forms on iron and steel, caused by the air when it is not completely dry
strand, threads put together to form a rope or a wire
occult, secret, meaning that which is outside the laws or forces of nature

'Mr Arengo-Smythe!' the Judge was becoming angry. 'Who on earth do you think you're talking to?'

'No one on earth, my Lord. It's White Owl. He always wants to have his say. There's no keeping him quiet.'

'Who is this White Owl?' the Judge stared at me. 'Do you know, Mr Rumpole?' 5

'Oh, yes, my Lord. White Owl is a Sioux Indian who, unhappily, lost his life at the battle of Little Big Horn.'

'Well, tell your client to *get rid* of him at once. I'm not having him here. This is a court of law, Mr Rumpole. Not 10 a darkened sitting-room in Earl's Court. Now, then. What's your case? Where do you say the voice came from?'

Ever ready with a well-known *quotation*, I was able to answer: 'There are more things in heaven and earth than 15 are dreamed of in your *philosophy*.'

'Members of the Jury, the question you have to answer is: did Mr Arengo-Smythe intend to *deceive*? My client has told you that he knew the line between the two rooms was broken. But the voice of White Owl was coming from 20 somewhere. From where, Members of the Jury? That is the question you have to ask yourselves. Is it just possible that the Sioux had entered that little sitting-room? Or is it possible that my client truly believed that he had? Either way, Members of the Jury, the Prosecution hasn't 25

get rid of, to make go away
quotation, a person's words as repeated by someone else. This quotation is from Shakespeare's Hamlet, 1.5. (Hamlet to Horatio.)
philosophy, here, that which is generally believed about existence; a person's view of life and death
deceive, to cause people to believe something which is false

proved its case and Mr Arengo-Smythe must be *acquitted.*'

I made the best speech I could and the Judge *summed up* nervously. Someone, he pointed out, had spoken in 5 the darkened sitting-room. If it was not the microphone, as now seemed certain, was it Mr Arengo-Smythe performing an act of *ventriloquism*? If it were his voice, did he honestly believe that he was possessed by some spirit who had died many years ago? Or had this been an 10 example of the occult taking place? The Jury must remember that even Mr Rumpole had not suggested that any of White Owl's *predictions* had proved correct. His *Lordship* then left the matter in their hands and popped out of court for a cup of tea and a breath of fresh air. 15 Whether it was because of me or White Owl, our day was crowned with success. The jury was not *convinced* of my client's guilt and he was acquitted by Mr Justice Teasdale, who seemed delighted to be shot of the whole business.

When we parted in the Old Bailey entrance, Arengo- 20 Smythe came close to me and spoke unusually quietly. 'I never used White Owl's voice, Mr Rumpole,' he said. 'I *swear* I never.'

'But you knew the wire was not connected?'

'No, Mr Rumpole. I'm sorry to say I did not.'

acquit, to find not guilty
sum up, to give the main points, here of evidence in a trial
ventriloquism, "speech from the stomach", that is the act of speaking without moving the lips
prediction, something which has been foretold, that is declared in advance to happen in the future
Lordship, form of address, here to a judge
convince, to make someone believe something
swear, to declare or promise in a very serious way

'Don't tell me anymore.' I wanted to get rid of the man as quickly as possible, but he went on. 'But I must tell you. I thought White Owl was Harriet, honestly I did. Where was he coming from?'

He looked at me, clearly frightened, but I had no comfort for him. 5

'The other side, as you would call it, if you're now telling the truth.'

'It must be. Oh, Mr Rumpole. It must be so. I don't know how I'm going to manage. I'm frightened.' 10

'Tell me' – I couldn't spare much sympathy for the man, but there was a question that had to be answered – 'I suppose that wire must have been broken when Mr and Mrs Ballard came to you to see into the future?'

'Must have been, Mr Rumpole. That was only a day or 15 two before we had the visit from the police.'

'And today,' I remembered, 'is the 14th of December.'

'There was a black cloud over it, White Owl said. Something terrible is sure to happen. Oh, do warn Mr Ballard, please. Do give him a serious warning.' 20

And then Mr Arengo-Smythe, looking extremely fearful, walked out of my life. In fact he walked out of life, full stop. That afternoon, as I read in my evening paper, he *stumbled* and fell from the platform of the Bank tube station in front of an advancing train. White Owl had 25 been quite correct about the black cloud hanging over that day. Soapy Sam, however, remains Head of our Chambers and the downstairs loo has, at last, been dragged into the twentieth century.

| *stumble*, to catch the foot against something when walking

Rumpole and the *Reform* of Joby Jonson

'Rumpole. **Rumpole**!' She Who Must Be Obeyed woke me up with a loud whisper. 'Can you hear something?'
'Hear what?'
'Sounds. Someone is in the flat.'
5 '**We're** in the flat. We usually are at night.' I couldn't hear anything except the usual noises that the central-heating system gives off during the night. 'Don't be afraid, Hilda,' I said to calm my wife's nerves. 'The flat is full of noises,
10 Sounds, and sweet airs, that give delight, and hurt not ...'
Hilda was silenced by Shakespeare, but a few seconds later She was at it again. 'You know who it is, don't you?'
'How would I know who it is?'
15 'So you admit it's someone.' A great cross-examiner was lost when Hilda didn't become a barrister. 'No doubt it's one of those you do business with.'
'What on earth do you mean?'
'It's some *burglar* or other.'
20 I tried to reason with her. I asked her why any half-way intelligent burglar would break into our flat for the sake of a few bottles of Pommeroy's *plonk*, a rented television set and her old friend Dodo Mackintosh's watercolour of a rainy afternoon in Lamorna Cove.
25 'I don't know, Rumpole.' Hilda thought the matter over. 'Why don't you go and see?'

reform, improvement; change from a bad to an honest character
burglar, person who breaks into a house to steal
plonk, cheap wine

The bed was warm, I'd had a hard day at the Bailey and was due for a harder one in the morning. 'No need to trouble the fellow,' I said weakly.

'Are you afraid to find out who it is?'

'Of course I'm not! I'm well known as an entirely fearless lawyer. I don't mind what I say to judges.'

'I don't believe it's a judge in there. The point is, are you afraid of burglars?'

'It's not a burglar, Hilda. You're imagining things.'

'All right, then prove it.'

'I can't, I'm asleep.'

'Or is that another job you'd rather leave to a woman?' She climbed out of bed and went off to battle.

Well, there are limits. So I went after Hilda and entered our sitting-room. It seemed to be burglar-free, the television set was still with us and Dodo's view of Lamorna Cove had found no takers. However, the window was open by the table where I had left a brief.

'You see, Rumpole, the window's open.' She thought it proved her case.

'Didn't we leave it open?'

'I'm not sure.'

'We'd make the most terrible witnesses. But this is rather *odd*.' I was looking at my brief in the case of the Queen against Joby Jonson, accused of robbery with *violence* of a seventy-five-year-old lady in the Euston area. Working on the papers before we went to bed I had left them, as I usually do, all over the table and in no particular order. Now they had been put together.

odd, strange
violence, (act of) great force causing harm

Hilda was going through the *drawers*. 'Nothing's missing.'

'Something is.'

'What?' 'The paper regarding the evidence of Joby
5 Jonson, the sixteen-year-old robber of old-age *pensioners*. His defence, such as it is, has disappeared into thin air.'

'So somebody **was** here.' Hilda was right. She usually is.

At that time, when crime arrived at Froxbury Mansions, Claude Erskine-Brown was waiting, in a state of mind
10 going from high spirits to loss of hope, to discover

Hilda opens a drawer

pensioner, person who has retired from work and receives a sum of money regularly from the government

whether the *Lord Chancellor* had given him a silk *gown* and permitted him to write the letters Q.C. after his name. If you want to become Her Majesty's Counsel you have to apply, with the support of a few judges, and wait patiently for the answer. 5

So the morning after our *burglary*, the Erskine-Browns were at breakfast in their fancy Islington house. As Phillida was reading The Times,* the conversation, I should guess from my knowledge of the events that followed, went something like this. 10

'Any sort of news in the paper today, Philly?' Claude would ask.

Lord Chancellor, the head of the English legal system
gown, see picture. A barrister is allowed to wear a silk gown when appointed Queen's Counsel.
burglary, the act of breaking into a house to steal
*newspaper

'Some sort of news, yes,' his wife told him. 'Danger of war in Bulgaria ... '

'No, I mean important news. The list of the new Q.C.s, for example.'

5 'Look for yourself.' Phillida offered him The Times, but sudden fear seized him. 'No, Philly. I'm not brave enough to look myself. I couldn't put up with another *disappointment*.' The truth of the matter is that Claude had applied for Silk five years running, and his name had not yet 10 appeared on the list. Now Phillida read out: 'The list of Queen's Counsel will be *announced* by the Lord Chancellor next month.'

'Nothing to say I'll get it?' Claude asked.

'Nothing to say you won't. I mean you've asked often 15 enough.'

'We all know you got it first time.' His tone may have become somewhat bitter.

'Rather a *fluke*, actually.'

'It wasn't a fluke. It was because you're a woman. It's 20 a bit hard being *discriminated* against all the time for reasons of sex.'

Sixteen-year-old Joby Jonson was in *custody*. He was on *remand*, *awaiting* trial, a person still not proven guilty. He was banged up with adult criminals in an *overcrowded*

disappointment, feeling of failure when you do not get what you have been looking forward to
announce, to make known publicly
fluke, a chance success
discriminate, to treat (a certain kind of people) differently
custody, care or guard of the police or prison authorities
on remand, sent back to prison until the trial can begin
await, wait for
overcrowded, having too many people in it

place which, through no particular fault of the prison *staff*, had become a university of crime. Prisoners on remand enjoy worse conditions than they did in the last century.

We sat in the interview room awaiting his arrival. 5

Our client was a short, *ginger-haired* youth. He sat down with his arms crossed and an unfriendly expression on his face. When he spoke he pointed his finger in my direction and called me "yo", a word that I finally was to translate as "you". 10

The events which led up to our meeting were as follows. On the morning of October 19th a Mrs Louisa Parsons, aged seventy-five, living at 1 Pondicherry Avenue, somewhere behind Euston Station, answered a ring at her front door. The youth who was there said, 'You 15 still living here, Mrs Parsons?' and ran off. Later that day a person she *identified* as the same youth, although his face was *partially* covered, again rang her doorbell. When she answered it he forced his way in, attacked her and hit her in the face and stomach. He then tied her up, kicked 20 her and, having broken some of the furniture, left with Mrs Parsons's post-office savings book, in which there was the sum of £5.79. She later identified Joby at an *identification parade* in the Euston nick. 'First time I ever see that silly old woman,' my client told me when I had 25 explained the case against him, 'was at the I.D. parade.'

staff, group of people, here working in the prison
ginger-haired, with red hair
identify, to (claim to) recognize (someone) as being a certain person
partially, not completely
identification parade, line-up of people arranged by the police to allow a witness to identify a suspect

I asked Bernard for a copy of our client's statement, the *document* which had disappeared from Froxbury Mansions in the middle of the night. Our defence, if you could call it that, was an *alibi*. The statement started in a not very promising way with, 'So far as I can remember, at the time Mrs Parsons was attacked I was hanging out near the loo in Euston station with three girls down from Manchester I found singing and dancing a bit. I think one of their names might have been Tina. I am unable to supply the full names and addresses of any of these persons.'

'Not a very good alibi.' I had to be honest about it.

'Can't you get me off on that?'

'I can't make much use of a so-called alibi which fails to explain the most important piece of evidence in this case.'

'What's that meant to be then?'

'Your fingerprints,' I had to tell him. 'On Mrs Parsons's front door. How did they get there?'

'How would I know?'

'Think about it,' I adviced him. 'It's a question you'll have to answer some time.'

'Mr Rumpole is going to do his very best for you.' Mr Bernard was always very reassuring. 'You listen to him, Joby.'

'And yo listen to me.' Joby's finger pointed at me. 'I'm not putting my hands up in court. I don't care what anyone says. Yo get that into your heads. Both of yo!'

As we were waiting for the prison gates to be opened for

document, written statement giving information, proof, evidence or the like
alibi, fact or statement showing that you were not there when the crime happened

us, Mr Bernard, who rarely expresses an opinion on a client, went so far as to say that he hadn't found our latest customer a particularly *likeable* young man. I quite agreed.

5 I had never been inside the *Home Office* before. I knew it only as a *threatening institution* which had managed, whether by bad luck or bad judgement, to turn prisons into *slums* and raise us to the proud position of number one of the European nations for sending our fellow 10 citizens to prison. I discovered a huge, grey building near St James's Park tube station. Inside I was met by a smiling young lady who invited me to take a seat in a waiting-room.

Finally I was admitted into a large room, full of sunlight 15 and modern paintings, and into the presence of a man who introduced himself as 'Tom Mottram, *Under-Secretary* for Home Affairs, with special responsibility for prisons. I'm the fellow who tries to keep your clients in.'

'Horace Rumpole,' I told him. 'I'm the fellow who tries 20 to keep them out.'

'Oh, good. Very good!' Mr Mottram seemed to be easily amused and he called on a pale little man to join

likeable, pleasing
Home Office, the department of state which deals with what happens within the country, for instance matters of law and order, care and education, etc.
threatening, giving warning about something bad that may happen
institution, here, public office
slum, group of houses, blocks or flats etc. where the conditions are dirty and overcrowded
Under-Secretary, head of ministry (department of Government)

in the fun. 'Isn't that good, Gladwyn? This is Gladwyn Dodds, *Parliamentary Private Secretary*. I say, Rumpole, sit yourself down. You may have wondered why I asked you to drop in.' Tom Mottram sat down beside me. 'It's about a young man called . . . ' He paused as though to search his memory for the name and then came out with 'Joby Jonson'. 5

'Really?'

'I'm a *constituency* M.P. I hope a good one.' Tom Mottram told me. 'Well, Joby Jonson's mother has come to see me, week in and week out, poor woman. She's really quite worried.' 10

'I expect she is.'

'I told the old girl I'd make sure he was properly defended. Of course, I was delighted to hear you were appearing for her. So I can tell my *constituent* he's being looked after?' 15

'He's having the time of his young life. Banged up twenty-three hours a day in a seven-foot cell with a couple of young criminals. And he's entirely innocent.' 20

'Innocent?' The Under-Secretary looked surprised. 'Is that your view of the matter?'

'Innocent as we all are,' I reminded him, 'until twelve fellow citizens come back into court and find us guilty.'

'Oh. You're showing us how you address the court.' Mottram smiled. 'It's good, isn't it, Gladwyn?' 25

Parliamentary Private Secretary, helper of government minister in his department
parliamentary, of *Parliament*, body of persons (members of Parliament) elected by the people of a country to make laws
constituency, (the *voters* in) a district which sends a member to Parliament; *voter*, see note, page 70
M.P., member of Parliament
constituent, person living in a constituency

'I was just trying to point out the condition of prisoners on remand.'

'Worse than they were a hundred years ago! We know that, don't we Gladwyn?'

5 'Only too well, I'm afraid, Mr Rumpole. And our Minister would be the first to agree with you.'

'So why doesn't your Minister do something about it?' I asked.

'The great British *voter*,' the Under-Secretary said.
10 'Terribly interested in seeing people banged up and terribly against them being let out. You know how over-crowded our prisons are. You know they don't do the slightest good. Gladwyn and I know it. Our Minister knows it. *Unfortunately* we have to obey our voters. So
15 we find it better to leave these things with people like you, and Seb Pilgrim!'

'And who?' The name meant nothing to me.

'You don't know Seb? He runs Y.P.R.T.'

'I beg your pardon?'

20 'Youth Programme Reform *Trust*,' Gladwyn explained. 'You must have heard of Sir Sebastian Pilgrim!'

'An absolutely splendid chap. He does wonderful things for hopeless cases like Joby Jonson. He teaches young lads *cricket*, gives them a bit of pride in themselves,
25 reforms their characters. You two should get together. You and Seb Pilgrim have your hearts in the right place.' Then the telephone rang and Gladwyn said the Minister would like a word with his Under-Secretary.

voter, person who votes or has the right to vote
unfortunately, unluckily
trust, here, arrangement by which money is given to a person to use in a particular way
cricket, famous English outdoor game played by two sides of eleven persons each

'Excuse us, won't you?' Tom Mottram went to the telephone. 'Our Master's Voice. Many thanks for dropping in. I'm sure you'll see young Jonson doesn't do anything *stupid* in court.'

'Stupid?' I asked as I got up.

'Make things worse for himself putting up some sort of foolish defence. I've told his poor old mother you've got a lot of experience in these sorts of cases.'

The Under-Secretary was now talking respectfully down the telephone and the audience was over.

When I opened the front door of the flat that night, after only half a bottle, at the most, of Pommeroy's Château Thames Embankment, I suffered a nervous shock. The air was torn by a terrible sound that I haven't heard since the nights of the *Blitz* when the Germans were overhead. Then Hilda appeared, pressed a number of *buttons* on some device fixed in our hallway and we had the *All Clear.*

'If it's going off every night,' I told her, 'I'll get a camp-bed put up in Chambers.'

'Don't be silly, Rumpole! It's a perfectly simple burglar

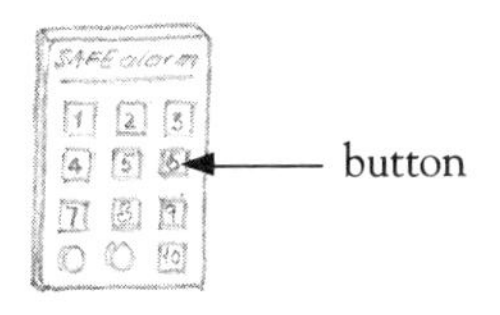

stupid, foolish
Blitz, sudden attack from the air (of British cities by the German airforce in 1940 and 1941)
All Clear, sound telling that the danger is over (expression from the war)

alarm. It's become absolutely necessary since the night of the crime. You just press seven, six, nine, oh, two, three, one, eight and the yellow button twice. Then it'll be quiet immediately.'

5 We were also being protected by a member of the Old Bill. He came out of the sitting room at that moment and introduced himself as Detective Sergeant Appleby of the Kensington force. He had been called in by She Who Must Be Obeyed in the great brief burglary case. 'Your 10 good lady seems to know my job better than I do,' D.S. Appleby said, 'tells me we must look for fingerprints.'

'I don't imagine you'll find any prints,' I told him rather sharply. I was in no mood for joking after the shock of the alarm. 'He must have been a professional.'

15 'And he didn't take anything of value, as I understand it, sir. Just some papers out of one of your cases? Now, I wonder who can have been interested in that?'

'Yes, Sergeant, I've been wondering that too.'

The case of Joby Jonson was receiving wide attention, 20 from the criminals to the corridors of power. A couple of evenings later I got a telephone call from none other than Sir Sebastian Pilgrim. He would simply love me to come down to the club and see the sort of work he was doing for lost sheep like young Joby, and, if I'd be good 25 enough to agree, he'd send his driver for me.

A few evenings later a Rolls Royce appeared in the Gloucester Road. I was driven in an easterly direction by a *chunky* man with a short haircut who introduced himself as Fred Bry, Sir Sebastian's driver. As we travelled

| *chunky*, solid and strong

along the Marylebone Road towards Euston Station, it was clear he was proud of his position, and he spoke of his employer as a great gentleman with a true understanding of *delinquent lads*. 'Never talks down to them, if you know what I mean. I've seen lads come to our club that you wouldn't think fit for anywhere except prison and they've ended up *reasonable* human beings, and pretty useful opening *bats*.' Fred wore no driver's uniform but was dressed like a sports *instructor*, in a high-necked *sweater* and *trainers*.

The Youth Programme Reform Trust or Y.P.R.T., as the Under-Secretary at the Home Office had called it, occupied an old building in Eversholt Street, near to the station. I was led down a stone staircase and then into a huge room. There was a coffee bar on our side of the room and a *ping-pong*, and, at the far end, a net had been fixed up. A line of boys were sending a ball to a tall, good-looking man with dark hair touched with grey, who had a cricket bat in his hand.

'Seb's what we call him,' Fred the driver told me as we walked up to the net. Seb came to greet me with his bat under his arm.

'Do you want to have a go in the net, Mr Rumpole?'

'Not in the least,' I told him.

delinquent, guilty of wrong-doing
lad, boy
reasonable, acting with good sense
bat, piece of wood for striking the ball in cricket; here batsman, person who strikes the ball in cricket
instructor, person who teaches a skill
sweater, pullover
trainers, sports shoes
ping-pong, table tennis

'Well, then perhaps you would like a drink?'

Seb handed his bat to a delinquent lad and we went over to the bar, where another delinquent was serving his fellows. 'Tea, coffee, hot soup, Seven-Up?'

'I thought you were offering me a drink? Now, if you have a glass of wine?'

'I'm afraid I haven't.' He was still smiling. 'I'll get you a coffee. And let's find ourselves a table.'

So, as you may imagine, I wasn't in a very happy mood as I sat and looked round the *gym*. Fred the driver was now seated in the middle of a circle of delinquents, talking to them. All the youths in the room, I noticed, were wearing dark sweaters, jeans and trainers, so they looked as though they were in a kind of uniformed group.

'I don't make the rules,' Seb told me when he came back with two plastic cups. 'The boys do. No alcohol, no smoking and no *drugs*. How's the coffee?'

'Is it coffee? I beg its pardon. I thought it was the soup.'

'I'm afraid this is the best we can do, Mr Rumpole. We've got more important things to think about.'

'Joby Jonson, for instance.' I brought him to the subject which was in so many minds.

'Well, yes. To be quite honest with you I'm worried about Joby. What we find here is that the first step to reform is to admit you're guilty. If only to your friends. Or at least to admit it to yourself. Look over there, in what we call our quiet corner.' The circle round Fred was paying attention to every word he said. 'What is it? A prayer meeting?' I asked. 'Something like that.' Seb was

gym, room used for exercise
drug, habit-forming substance dangerous to health, sometimes used as medicine as it brings relief from pain and worries

still smiling. 'The young lads there are coming out with all their crimes and wrong-doings. They talk them through. And then Fred Bry tells them where that sort of *conduct* leads to.'

'Your driver tells them?' 5

'Fred should know. He'd just come out of six years for robbery when I found a job for him.'

So I looked again at the group. One of the youths was talking, pouring his heart out, and Fred was listening patiently, nodding his head from time to time. 10

'So you think it's good for the soul to *confess*?' I asked Seb.

'Don't you?'

'Perhaps, but it's not particularly good for keeping you out of the nick.' 15

'Oh come on, Mr Rumpole. You can't believe Joby's innocent. Is he going to try and put up some sort of defence, I mean apart form the alibi?'

'Which alibi, exactly?' Seb, it seemed, followed the case stories of all his delinquents. 20

'Three strange girls from Manchester at the railway station dancing and singing songs outside the lavatory.'

'You know that's his story?'

'Of course, the lads all talk about each other's cases. But it's not highly probable, is it?' 25

'One thing I have learned, after almost half a century down the Old Bailey, is that the improbable is perfectly likely to happen.'

'I'm sure you want to help Joby.' Now Seb had become serious, so I gave him a serious answer. 'It's my job to help 30

conduct, the way in which something is managed or done
confess, to admit that you are guilty

him, not to decide his case. I might even manage to get him off.' But Seb's ideas of helping clients were a little different from mine. 'If you could get him to admit what he's done, if you could get him to face up to it and not tell silly lies, that would really help him on his way back to reality.'

'And to about six years in the nick.' I had to point out the downside of confessing.

'He came here often over the last two years. I refuse to consider him one of my failures. I'm sure we both want to do our best for him. Tell me how I can help.'

'I suppose I could call you as a character witness.'

'Count on me, Mr Rumpole!' He seemed delighted to offer his services. 'You can count on me.'

'Thank you very much. Now if you'll forgive me, I have an important meeting.'

So Fred Bry pointed the Rolls in the direction of Froxbury Mansions and a much-needed bottle of Château Thames Embankment.

'That Joby Jonson's been a terrible disappointment to all of us,' the driver said. 'I knew he was going wrong when I heard he was hanging round the station. It's where they pick up the drugs that kids bring down from the North. It leads them to do terrible inhuman things. We did our best with Joby, Seb and I. We both tried hard. It's over to you now, Mr Rumpole. Get the lad to face up to what he's done, it's the only way.'

When I was in the clerk's room a day or so later and found myself alone with Dot, our *typist*, she said that she wanted to ask my advice. 'It's about my dad. The thing is,

1 *typist*, one who uses a typewriter (a writing machine)

they want to do some new building down his street, but he won't sell his house. He says he's too old to move now anyway, and he told them so. What he wants to know is, is there any way they can get him out, legally, I mean?'

I had to admit to her that property law wasn't exactly my strong side, but I'd make inquiries and let her know. Then I asked her exactly where Mr Clapton lived. 'MacGlinky Terrace,' she said. 'Off Eversholt Street, behind Euston Station. Do you know the area?' I did and I had a feeling that what Dot had just told me added something to my knowledge.

When I got home I found Hilda reading the Daily Telegraph* by the gas-fire and she was delighted to tell me that there was a long article in it of "my friend".'

'Really. Which friend is that?'

'Well, not one of the criminal classes certainly. Someone you ought to be proud of. You might invite him round to dinner so I could meet him.'

'Invite who round to dinner, Hilda?'

'Sir Sebastian Pilgrim. He spends his time trying to reform young criminals. And it seems that Seb – everyone calls him Seb – is an excellent businessman as well. Chairman of something called Maiden Over *Holdings*. I don't know why you're not Chairman of anything, Rumpole.'

'Maiden Over? What's that exactly?'

'Some sort of property company. He started it with Tom Mottram, M.P. Of course, now Mottram's a member of the Government he's had to give up his position in the company.'

*newspaper
holding(s), property owned; here part of a name of a company owning property (land and houses)

'Go on, Hilda. I'm finding your Daily Telegraph talk unusually interesting.'

'It says here that Seb believes in Britain. "I have faith in the future of this country,"' Hilda read from the article, '"which is why we're building a large hotel and a shopping centre in the area of – "' The doorbell rang. It was D.S. Appleby, who had at last found time to come and dust our sitting room with fingerprint powder. It wasn't until after he had done the job, been given a cup of tea and sent on his way that I was able to pick up the newspaper and discover where Sir Sebastian's faith in our country was going to find expression. It was just behind Euston Station.

Phillida Erskine-Brown had managed to get Soapy Sam Ballard to invite her to lunch. How exactly she played her hand I can only guess.

'You know,' Phillida probably began as soon as the order was placed, 'I've been longing to talk to you about Claude. He's not at all that easy to live with these days. The trouble is that he believes that if he were a woman he might do better with the Lord Chancellor. What do you think of that?'

'I think that's very silly.' Ballard had no doubt about it.

'So do I.' And then she gave him the honest and wide-eyed look which had such a wonderful effect on juries, and asked him directly, the wine having no doubt been poured, 'Don't you think Claude ought to get Silk?'

'No, I do not. That would mean we had three Silks in Chambers, and there wouldn't be enough really important work for three leaders.'

She smiled at him. 'You were thinking entirely of me,

weren't you. You thought I'd get fewer *leading briefs* with Claude as a rival. But I want you to be the first to know I shan't be looking for leading briefs in the future.'

'You won't?'

'I'm leaving the *Bar*.' 5

'Phillida!'

'I've made up my mind. Don't look so sad, Sam. We'll still be able to meet for lunch. And you know, it might make it easier for us if Claude were really busy and away doing leading briefs for long periods of time. We could 10 have lunch together often. You'd like that, wouldn't you?'

'Well, as a matter of fact, Phillida, I believe I would.'

'Then just lift the telephone to dear old Keith in the Lord Chancellor's office. Tell him that Claude ought to 15 get Silk, even though he is a man through absolutely no fault of his own.'

I had a harder struggle ahead than the Erskine-Brown struggle for Silk. Joby Jonson's future was in my hands. Mr Justice Graves had been put in charge of the case and 20 no less than Phillida Erskine-Brown, Q.C., who could turn the head of our Head of Chambers, was in charge of the prosecution. Joby Jonson, attacker and robber of grandmothers, came to stand for all that was bad in British youth. 25

I gave Mr Bernard his battle orders. He was to get in touch with Mr Clapton of MacGlinky Terrace, near Euston Station, and discover if that address might be

leading brief, case which may serve as a guide or rule in deciding future cases
Bar, here, the profession of barrister

anywhere near Pondicherry Avenue, home of the attacked old lady. I also needed as much information as possible on the business of Maiden Over Holdings and about any *estate agents* they might employ. The faithful
5 Bernard wrote everything down carefully.

'I don't know if you've had any experience of Mr Justice Graves?'

'As a matter of fact I've never been before him.'

'Then, my dear, you must have led a charmed life.'

10 We were standing side by side, Mrs Erskine-Brown and I, as the old Gravestone swept on to the bench like an *icy* wind. We bowed to each other and then went through the opening *formalities*.

Phillida Erskine-Brown was opening the Prosecution
15 case. 'Members of the Jury,' she spoke to them in her most charming voice, 'we say that Jonson paid two visits to Number 1 Pondicherry Avenue that day. He came in the morning and asked Mrs Parsons if she were still living there. When he found out she was, he returned that
20 afternoon, having made some attempts at covering his face. He attacked this lady, old enough to be his grand-mother, and robbed her of what were no doubt her small lifetime's savings.'

'Five pounds, 79 pence,' I *murmured* from my seat.

25 'Did you say something, Mr Rumpole?' the Judge asked in an icy voice.

estate agent, person whose job is to sell houses and land
icy, very cold
formality, something which is done for appearance but has little meaning
murmur, to speak in a low voice

'I was just reminding my learned friend that the sum was exactly £5.79,' I rose to say politely.

'Mr Rumpole, I have no doubt we shall be hearing from you later. Now I think we might let Mrs Erskine-Brown open her case without any more *interruptions*. Yes, Mrs Erskine-Brown?' 5

'It remains to be seen, Members of the Jury,' she went on, 'what sort of defence, if any, will be put forward for Jonson. We have been given notice of an alibi which shows how lightly this very serious case is being taken, 10 both by the accused youth and by his learned Counsel, Mr Rumpole. It is alleged that while the attack was taking place, Jonson was, "dancing with some girls from Manchester outside the lavatory at Euston Station."'

After the opening speech, the victim of the attack, 15 Mrs Louisa Parsons, a bright-eyed old lady, entered the witness box. At the end of her evidence she was asked about the identification parade, on which occasion, she told us, the police had been very kind to her and saw she got a cup of tea. 20

'Did you then identify the youth who visited you twice on the 19th and attacked you on the second occasion?' Phillida asked. At this the old lady pointed to the *dock* and said, 'There he stands!' No prosecutor could have asked for more and I rose to cross-examine, knowing that 25 any attempt to shake Mrs Louisa Parsons would sink me with the Jury for ever.

I started as though addressing my own grandmother. 'Mrs Parsons, this £5.79 didn't represent your entire

interruption, the act of *interrupting*, that is stopping a person while he is saying or doing something
dock, here, the box in a law court where the accused sits or stands

wordly wealth, did it? Do you own your little house in Pondicherry Avenue?'

'My husband saved for it. Worked all his life as a clerk at the station. It was paid up by the time he died.'

'Have you not been offered a large sum of money for that little house?'

'I wasn't going to move no matter how often they asked me. It wasn't the money, you see. That was the home Mr Parsons meant me to have for my life. I wasn't moving.'

'Although they asked you very often?'

'I'm sick and tired of them always ringing me up,' she agreed, 'and sending me letters. Well, I said I'm not interested in selling. Not to you. Not to anybody.'

Faithful Bernard had called on Dot's father and made sure that MacGlinky Terrace did, in fact, lead off Eversholt Street and into Pondicherry Avenue. He had made copies of a number of letters Mr Clapton had received. I picked them up and asked Mrs Parsons, 'Did the letters come from a firm of estate agents called Jebber and Jonas?'

'They may have done. I never kept them.'

At this point Judge Graves interrupted my questioning. 'Mr Rumpole, what on earth has this information got to do with the charges against your client for robbery?'

'That is something you may discover, my Lord, if I am allowed to continue with my cross-exmination without interruption.' Having dealt with that I gave my full attention to the witness. 'You say that young Joby Jonson called in the morning and said, "You still living here, Mrs Parsons?"'

'Yes, he did.'

'Did you think that question might have some connec-

tion with the repeated *requests* to you to sell your house?'
Having thought it over, Mrs Parsons said, 'Not at the time, no.'

'Mr Rumpole, are you seriously suggesting that your client, accused of the robbery of £5.79, was working for a firm of estate agents?' 5

'I will *demonstrate* that they are both working for the same organization.' After which interruption I took up my conversation with the witness again. 'Later that day you say a young man rang at the door and when you opened it he attacked and robbed you.' 10

'I heard the bell. I thought, he's back again, I'll give him a piece of my mind.'

'You weren't frightened of him when you went to the door?' 15

'Not then, no. I was when I saw him, though. His head was covered.'

'You say in your statement that his face was hidden the second time he called.'

'It was hidden a bit, yes,' she had to admit. 20

'Mrs Parsons, can you be sure it was the same boy?'

She was silent for a moment. Then she said, 'I think it was the same.'

'You **think** so?'

'He had the same clothes – a dark sweater and jeans, training shoes – whatever they call them.' 25

'The uniform of thousands and thousands of young men all over London. But you didn't see his face?'

'Just the eyes. That was enough for me.'

'His eyes may have been enough for you, Mrs Parsons. 30

request, the act of asking (for something)
demonstrate, to show or point out clearly

They may not be enough for a jury to convict this young man on a serious charge of robbery with violence.' I gave the twelve honest citizens a long and searching look and sat down, quite content with myself.

5 After the first day's work was done I paid a visit to the cells under the Old Bailey.

'The time has come for you to tell the truth, Joby. Confessing is good for the soul. Now I want you to admit that someone told you to go round to the old lady's house
10 and ask her if she was still living there. That was in the morning. What were you doing in the afternoon?'

'I told you. Didn't I.'

'Yes, and for once I believe you. You had taken an *Ecstacy* pill you bought off some girls down from
15 Manchester – an activity which led you to go dancing and singing outside the lavatory in Euston Station and later to feeling really bad with a certain loss of memory.'

'How comes yo know so much about doing an "E"?'

'How come I know so much about everything? I know
20 you went to the house in the morning because your fingerprints were on the door and Mrs Parsons saw you. That was why she picked you out at the I.D. parade. I know you didn't go in the afternoon because the group you work for were so interested in discovering our
25 defence. They are very much afraid you'll say another of their lads came after you and did the serious business. Well, you'll have to tell the truth, Joby, before this case is over.' I sat down opposite him then and saw him stare at his feet. He didn't lift his eyes to ask, 'What's this group
30 yo's on about then?'

I *ecstacy*, (feeling of) very great joy. Here, a name given to a drug

'Don't play games with me. You know damn well who I'm talking about. You can start telling us the truth tomorrow.' Then we left our client with a certain amount of relief and Mr Bernard went off to arrange the presence of a witness on whom I placed our few remaining hopes.

The next morning I asked the judge if I might call a character witness, a particularly busy man, to give his evidence before my client Jonson went into the witness-box. When the old Gravestone heard that my witness was none other than the well-known believer in Britain, Sir Sebastian Pilgrim, he did not object and neither did Phillida.

So Seb entered the witness-box. When he admitted he was Sir Sebastian Pilgrim, Graves gave him a big smile. 'And do you run an organization called the Youth Programme Reform Trust, allegedly to help boys who have fallen into criminal ways?' I asked him.

'Sir Sebastian, your wonderful work with Y.P.R.T. is well known to many of us.' Graves continued to butter up the witness, who wasn't entirely delighted with the form of my question.

'I do run that organization to help delinquent boys,' he said. 'I don't know why Mr Rumpole used the word "allegedly"'.

'Perhaps if I go on a little my meaning may become clear.' And I asked Seb, 'Are you also chairman of Maiden Over Holdings, which is planning a development near Euston Station that includes building a large hotel and a tourist shopping-centre?'

'I am.'

'And aren't you having trouble with certain householders who refuse to sell their homes to make way for

this great and splendid development?'

'No, I don't think so. Not particularly.'

'Are you not? Do you not employ, among others, estate agents called Jebber and Jonas?' There was a pause as the witness seemed to be searching his memory. Then he said, as lightly as possible, 'The name sounds familiar.'

'Please answer the question. Do you employ them or not?'

'From time to time.' Seb's smile to the jury seemed to be saying, 'It couldn't matter less,' but I asked the *usher* to

usher, officer or servant in a court of law

hand him one of the estate agent's letters to Mr Clapton. 'Is this a letter from that firm to a Mr Peter Clapton of MacGlinky Terrace, asking him to sell his house to make room for a new hotel development?'

'That would seem so.' Seb hardly looked at it.

'Is it your hotel development?'

'Well, I can't think of anyone with such plans.'

'And isn't Mrs Parsons of 1 Pondicherry Avenue also a householder who won't sell to your company?'

'She might be.' Had I been Phillida I would have interrupted long before this, for I was breaking all rules by treating my own character witness with growing *hostility*. When she did rise, I knew it was useless to argue. 'Of course,' I surprised her, 'my learned friend is perfectly right. This is a character witness and I will come at once to my client's character. Sir Sebastian, do you take the view that young delinquents should admit what they've done and tell the truth about it?'

'Yes, I believe that's the start of reform.' Seb looked safely back on his home ground.

'Sir Sebastian, do you really want Joby Jonson to tell the truth about this case?'

'Yes, indeed.'

'He came to your club having been in trouble over a few minor matters. No violence in his record?'

'I think it was only theft.'

'And you hoped to reform him?'

'I always hope, and I thought there was some good in the lad. He turned up regularly in the club. I felt I might make quite a useful cricket player out of him.'

| *hostility*, ill will; lack of friendliness

'Did you also hope to turn him into a useful young man to *terrorize* Mrs Parsons into selling her house to your company?'

'My Lord, that's the most *outrageous* suggestion! Mr Rumpole is cross-examining his own witness.' Phillida got up again and, surprise, surprise, his Lordship was on her side. 'Mrs Erskine-Brown, I completely agree. That is a question that should never have been asked, as you must know perfecly well, Mr Rumpole.'

'My Lord, I think it only fair that I should be allowed to answer Mr Rumpole. There is no truth in it at all.'

'No truth in it at all.' Graves repeated the words to himself and wrote them down carefully. 'Spoken, if I may say so, like a great sportsman. Mr Rumpole, you will limit yourself to questions about your client's character.'

'Delighted, my Lord. Sir Sebastian, did you then realize that young Joby Jonson was not completely to be trusted? Trusted enough to send with a final warning before lunch perhaps, but the afternoon attack had to be done by another of your lads, with his face hidden.'

'Mr Rumpole!' Mr Justice Graves shouted. 'I will not have any more of this. I stopped you before but you continue in attempting to *involve* this gentleman in the terrible crime of which your client stands accused. That is not the way in which we "play the game" in these courts, as you should know perfectly well.'

'I'm extremely sorry, my Lord.' I managed my most

terrorize, to make very frightened by using or threatening violence
outrageous, terrible
involve, to cause (a person) to take part (in an activity)

charming smile. 'I've never entirely understood the rules of cricket.'

Outside the court just before lunch I saw Ballard talk to the Prosecuting Counsel telling her that he had "done it".

'Done what exactly?' Phillida didn't seem to understand.

'Seen old Keith from the Lord Chancellor's office. I said that we would be very pleased to see Claude getting Silk. So what about lunch? I know a very nice place.'

'Sorry, Ballard, I think I'm going to be rather too busy for lunches in the near future.'

Phillida had won her case, but I wasn't so sure that I was going to win mine. My cross-examination of the great sportsman had been the high point. Then I had to call Joby and, although he told the truth as I had put it to Sir Sebastian, he wasn't the sort of witness the Jury could ever fall in love with and Phillida was very clever in bringing out his many bad qualities.

As always I felt a great relief when my client had left the witness box and returned to the silence of the dock. Now it was up to me. 'Members of the Jury.' I began my final speech. 'Perhaps now, young Joby Jonson has taken the first step on the road to reform by telling you the truth. Until he went into that witness-box he was protecting his boss, his gang leader, the well-known cricketer. But the much-loved Seb Pilgrim had no intention of protecting him. He used Joby to play a small part in a plan to terrorize an innocent old lady into selling her house. And then he was content to see him locked up for years for the crime **he** planned.'

When my speech was over I sat down and felt a great weight lift from my shoulders. I had done my job as well as I could, and now it was up to the honest twelve to make a decision. His Lordship, during his summing up, had made it clear what he would like that decision to be. After a couple of hours in their room the jury decided to agree with him and Joby Jonson was sentenced to go to prison for five years. During which time, I thought, if there were anything Joby did not know now about the life of crime, he would certainly have learned it. So he was taken down to the cells to continue his education.

One morning when we were all sitting in the clerk's room on the hunt for briefs, Claude Erskine-Brown came in, having at last had the courage to buy The Times, which he had opened on an inner page where the list of those fortunate to be crowned in Silk was printed.

'Hallo, there. Hallo, you chaps. Hallo, Liz. Good morning, Dot. Hi there, Henry! You've all seen The Times, of course. Great news isn't it, and completely unexpected. Seen it, have you, Rumpole? I shall be leading you, my dear old fellow. I shall be sitting in front of you, doing your next murder for you.'

'*Congratulations*,' Ballard said. 'It's wonderful news about your wife.'

'Philly?' Claude looked surprised. 'What about Philly?'

'Haven't you looked at the front page of that newspaper, Erskine-Brown? And the photograph.'

It seemed the poor fellow had left the house early, bought the paper at the Temple tube station and turned, with trembling fingers, immediately to the Silk list. Phillida had not told the rest of us, and certainly not her

congratulations, word to express pleasure and joy (to a person) at a happy event, a success he has had etc.

husband, that she was going to become a judge. Mrs Erskine-Brown was now about to take her place on the High Court bench and, as her photograph made clear, she was going to be a good deal easier on the eye than Mr Justice Graves.

'She never even told her clerk!' Henry said, and somewhere inside Ballard the penny finally dropped. 'So that's what she meant,' he told us, 'when she said she was leaving the Bar.'

When Erskine-Brown first stood up in court dressed in the full glory of his new-found Silk, he found himself bowing low and saying, 'if your Ladyship pleases,' and, 'with very great respect' to his wife. And I was to address Hilda in the same way when D.S. Appleby telephoned to tell me the result of the search for fingerprints She Who Must Be Obeyed had ordered. 'They found one,' I reported to her as we sat on either side of the gas-fire in our sitting-room, 'by the window over there. It was the thumb print of a criminal who was sent down for robbery with violence for at good many years. He now acts as driver to that great British cricketer and reformer of the young, Sir Sebastian Pilgrim. Fred Bry it was who entered our home by night. You know what that means, Hilda? It means that the case of Joby Jonson is not entirely over.'

'Then I'm glad I got the burglar alarm fitted. That's all I can say.'

'It's not all I can say, old thing. I'd like to say thank you for demanding the fingerprints to be taken. It shows how important it is to have a woman on the case.'

Questions

Rumpole and the Children of the Devil

1. What is Rumpole's position in Chambers?
2. How is the relation between Rumpole and his wife?
3. Who are the Timsons and the Molloys?
4. Why was Tracy removed from her home?
5. Describe the social worker.
6. In what way is the Juvenile Court different from a normal court?
7. What did Dominic Molloy tell the social worker?
8. How did the masks happen to be in Cary Timson's garage?
9. Why did the Molloys want to frame Tracy and her dad?
10. Why did Rumpole take dancing lessons?

Rumpole and the Soothsayer

1. Who is Sam Ballard?
2. Why would he want to look into the future?
3. How did Mr Arengo-Smythe become Rumpole's client?
3. What is he accused of?

4. What happens at the trial?
5. What was wrong with the 14th of December?
6. Have you ever had your future told?

Rumpole and the Reform of Joby Jonson

1. What is Joby Jonson accused of?
2. Why is Sir Sebastian interested in his case?
3. Describe his reform programme.
4. What is Maiden Over Holdings?
5. How is Dot Clapton's father connected with the case?
6. How does Rumpole build up Joby Jonson's defence?
7. How does the burglary at Rumpole's flat influence the case?
8. How did Claude Erskine-Brown finally earn his Silk?

Rumpole and the Children of the Devil

Prefixes

Write the correct prefix (un-, in-, im-, dis-,) in front of the following words. You can find them all in this story:

usual
faithful
effective
familiar
respectful
interested
directly
lawful
correct
decent
proper
experienced
possible
satisfied

Find examples in the other stories.

Improve your vocabulary.

Use other words for saying:

to occupy my mind (p. 5); to pick a fight (p. 7); stood his ground (p. 10); to take a more sinister turn (p. 10); Mirabelle produced a piece of paper (p. 13); to keep one's ear to the ground (p. 14); an extended family (p. 14); I had acted for Cary (p. 16); by bits and pieces (p. 18); I blew into the clerk's room (p. 20); Got it in one (p. 21); that shop that got done over (p. 24); to draw the line somewhere (p. 26); I should keep off the law (p. 31); That goes without saying (p. 32); being at a loss for an explanation (p. 32); The afternoon dragged on (p. 37); Hang about a bit (p. 39); was pure invention (p. 40); to have got the message (p. 40).

Possessive Case (Tracy's parents)
We add "'s" to a singular noun and "'" to a plural.
Irregular plurals have "'s" (children's).

Singular names (and nouns) ending in "-s" usually have possessive forms in "'s".

... of ... is mostly used when talking about things, and when the noun is immediately followed by a phrase.

Join the following two nouns:
Her Majesty/judges
devil/mask
conventional society/rules
Old Bill/footsteps
the Timsons/record of stealing
headmistress/office
Dominic/silence
Crockthorpe Local Authority/care
Miss Jones/unanswered question
Erskine Brown/face
corridor/end
Uncle Dennis/evidence
Miss Jones/smile
Children/Home
their daughter/hand

You may find the answers in the story.

Making nouns out of verbs:
Add -er to the verb: work – worker. There are several of such nouns, indicating a person, in this and the other stories. Find them. Make your own nouns from verbs in this story like 'sitting' (p. 5): (baby-)sitter. Add -ment to the verb: punish – punishment (the act of punishing). There are a few more of these nouns in the story. Can you find them? Do you know any others?

Rumpole and the Soothsayer

Improve your vocabulary.
In English it is very usual to place prepositions or adverbs after certain verbs which gives a variety of meanings: the Molloys did it over (p. 46), meaning 'robbed it'. Explain the following expressions:
calling off the arrangements (p. 47); to be put off (p. 47); get on with it (p. 47); to pass over (p. 51); Don't break in (p. 52); to catch up with (p. 54) You'll get him off (p. 54); I had hit upon (p. 55).
Give other examples that you can think of or have come across in these stories.

Rumpole and the Reform of Joby Jonson

Most *adverbs* are made from an adjective by adding -ly. For example usual – usually. An adverb tells us more about a verb, in what way someone does something or in what way something happens. We also use adverbs before adjectives and other adverbs, for example: an entirely fearless lawyer. There are several examples on each page of this story. A few words ending in -ly, however, are not adverbs but adjectives.
Decide whether the words in italics are right or wrong. Correct those which are wrong:

We *usual* are in the flat at night. _____
… and wait *patient* for the answer.
… with … an *unfriendly* expression on his face. _____
… his face was *partial* covered. _____
… that *silly* old woman. _____
… who *rarely* expresses an opinion. _____
(he) seemed to be *easy* amused. _____
(he) was talking *respectful* down the telephone. _____
It's a *perfectly* simple burglar alarm. _____
It's *perfectly likely* to happen. _____
… which shows how *light* this serious case is being taken.
_____
… you run an organization … *allegedly* to help boys …
_____
Did you hope to turn him into a *useful* young man. _____

Passive (be done/have been done ... by)
We often prefer the passive when it is not so important who did or what caused the action.
For example: Hilda was silenced by Shakespeare. Active: Shakespeare silenced Hilda.
Complete the following sentences with the verb in the correct passive form:
Now they __________ together. (active: he had put them) (p. 61)
The list of Queen's Counsel __________ by the Lord Chancellor. (he will announce it) (p. 64)
The air __________ by a terrible sound. (tore) (p. 71)
We __________ by a member of the Old Bill. (he was protecting us) (p. 72)
He __________ in by She Who Must Be Obeyed. (she had called him in) (p 72)
I __________ in an easterly direction by a chunky man. (he drove me) (p. 72)
the wine __________ (the waiter having poured it) (p. 78)
Mr Justice Graves __________ in charge of the case. (they had put him) (p. 79)
We __________ notice of an alibi. (they have given us) (p. 81)
she __________ about the identification parade. (they asked her) (p. 81)
Have you not __________ a large sum of money? (they have offered) (p. 82)

For your own notes: